# HANGIN' JUDGE

"You're either a very courageous man," Lunsford said, "or a very stupid one."

Morgan approached the judge's small desk. "While you're trying to figure out which, Judge, I suggest you hear what I have to say."

"I'm under no obligation to give an audience to a suspected fugitive."

Morgan once again drew and cocked the Colts. He leveled it at Lunsford's head and leaned a little forward when he spoke. "Yes, you are, Judge, in this case."

Morgan learned something at once about Judge Arlo Lunsford. He was not a man easily intimidated. He leaned back in his chair. "I can have you arrested or, if necessary, killed, Mr. Morgan, and when either one is done, no one will question me about it. If you live, you'll end up in Yuma prison. Killing me won't stop the process, except that if you lived, you'd hang."

# BUCKSKIN #20

# Pistol Grip

## Kit Dalton

LEISURE BOOKS    NEW YORK CITY

Dedicated with love to:
My Sis and her family
Marilyn, Bill and Billy Sturdivant
of
Miles City, Montana

A LEISURE BOOK

Published by

Dorchester Publishing Co., Inc.
6 East 39th Street
New York, NY 10016

Printed in the United States of America

# Pistol Grip

# 1

Lee Morgan rode into Cheyenne, Wyoming in the midst of a blizzard. He was cold, ass tired, hungry, irritated and damned near broke. The circumstances made for a very short temper and a potentially volatile situation.

He found a stall for his horse but Morgan's appearance prompted the liveryman to ask for payment in advance. Morgan couldn't blame him but it didn't do much for his attitude. It also made him wonder what he'd run into at the Cattlemen's Hotel.

"A single, three nights," Morgan said. He got the onceover from the desk clerk and Morgan heaved a sigh. "I'll give you one night in advance and the balance by checkout time." The clerk smiled and reversed the registration book.

The clerk scrutinized Morgan's signature for a moment and then looked up and smiled.

"That will be three dollars, sir." Morgan frowned. The clerk eyed him and then added, "I assume you wanted the bath included. Without the . . . ."

"Never mind," Morgan said, "the bath is fine." The clerk nodded. "The dining room will be open until six o'clock, Mr. Morgan."

"Yeah," Morgan said, picking up his gear, "thanks."

The room was plain. Morgan chuckled to himself. Just a few short weeks earlier, he'd been ensconced at the Brown Palace in Denver. Still, this was not the worst room he'd ever rented. He tossed his gear in the corner, pulled back the bed covers and the sheets. Nothing was crawling. He raised the window shade. It was a back room, not much of a view.

A single picture hung over the bed. It was crooked. Morgan hated crooked pictures. He straightened it and then looked at it. He chuckled again. It depicted a lone wolf atop a snow covered hill. It was howling at the moon. "I don't blame you, pal," Morgan said.

It was nearly four o'clock in the afternoon before Morgan woke up. He threw some cold water on his face and got dressed. He looked out of the window. It had stopped snowing. His circumstance was no better, but he sure as hell felt better. A shave, a bath and a few hours sleep gave him some of the energy he'd need to accomplish his next task. Figuring out what the hell he was going to do.

Morgan's luck at investments had always been on the down side. The Spade Bit ranch had floundered under his ownership, albeit an absentee ownership. He'd tried other things. A horse ranch which was raided, and the Spade Bit again, which was burned out. His most recent business venture had been in a stage line. At the outset it looked promising. Five months later the main office was nailed shut and one Jedediah Welsh had disappeared with what was left of Morgan's money. It was another chuckle. Welsh, thought Morgan, was a most appropriate name for his ex-business partner.

Morgan counted his money before he went to the dining room. If he paid two more days rent, ate light and got damned lucky in a poker game, he might get through the week. He'd come to Cheyenne with a plan in mind, however. The local cattlemen were growing more and more restless over the invasion of sheep. Several ranches had advertised for hired guns. Morgan wanted to check the validity of their claims, and if true, he'd hire his and he wouldn't hire cheap.

The beefsteak was good and Morgan topped off the meal by treating himself to a shot of good whiskey, the last in his own supply. He knew it might be a long dry spell. The idea of hiring his gun didn't bother him, he'd done that, in one form or another, most of his adult life. What did bother him was just how quickly he could do it. Many of the advertisements requested that letters be written to the ranchers. After all, it was winter and how much trouble were they having right now? Morgan was gambling on his skill and perhaps his reputation. He would try to hire on as a kind of gun hand's ramrod.

The casino proved to be another obstacle for Morgan. The smallest table stakes he could find were fifty dollars. Hell, he didn't have anywhere near fifty dollars. A house man told him he would have to come back on Monday night when there were several tables open to what the house man called, "penny ante" players.

Morgan considered bucking the cold weather and wandering around trying to find a game he could afford but the warmth of the bar changed his mind. That, and the fact the barkeep seemed to assume Morgan wanted his drinks charged to his room bill. He was told it was a new policy being instituted by many of the finer hotels in the country. Morgan decided he'd drink tonight and worry about the cost tomorrow.

"Just leave the bottle," Morgan said. The barkeep nodded.

Morgan returned to his room about nine o'clock. He was not drunk but the effects of the whiskey were evident. He read the evening paper and then simply sprawled out on his bed. A little more than an hour later, he was aroused by a gentle knock at the door. The whiskey hadn't dulled his senses or his reflexes that much and he was on his feet, gun drawn and far enough away from the door to avoid being shot.

"Yeah?" There was no reply but the knocking was repeated. "Who is it?"

"Please, sir, just let me in." The plea was whispered, the voice feminine. Morgan moved again, pressing his back against the wall next to the door.

"It's open." The girl came in and Morgan got a good look at her and made certain she was alone before he spoke. The girl's eyes were still adjusting to the semi-darkness, and when Morgan finally did say something the sound startled her.

"Who are you?" She blinked, looked down at the gun and stepped back. Morgan had forgotten about it. He holstered it. "Habit," he said. Then he repeated his question.

"Tamara Winfrey," came the reply. "I'm called Tammy."

"I won't bother introducing myself," Morgan said. "You either already know or you've got the wrong room. Which is it?"

"I know who you are and I've come to ask for your help."

"How do you know who I am and how did you know I was in Cheyenne?"

She smiled and relaxed a little. Morgan began to think she was somewhat older than she appeared. "May I sit down?"

"No need if you're not going to be here that long," Morgan said. He walked to her. "And you're not if I don't get some answers."

"Very well. I had a man, a man who worked for me, go to Fort Laramie to find you. You'd already left. He found out you were coming here and sent me a telegraph cable. Then he was

11

going to follow you and make the contact with you himself." She opened a small bag and produced the cable. Morgan read it and looked up.

"You said he was going to contact me. Where is he?"

"Dead." She winced a little and swallowed and licked her lips and said, "May I have a drink?"

"Of what?"

"Whiskey would be nice, if you have any left." Morgan eyed her, his head tilted to one side. "I saw you in the saloon. I saw the bottle."

Morgan didn't say anything but instead walked to the chiffonnier and poured the last two drinks from the bottle. He carried hers back to her and then silently held his glass out in a mock toast. They both drank. "Thank you," she said. Morgan nodded. "May I sit down now?"

"Who killed your man, and why?"

The girl sighed. "I know why," came the reply and then an added touch of disgust in the tone, "but if I knew who, I wouldn't be trying to hire you."

"And what makes you think I can be hired?"

"You're broke and you won't get on with anybody around here 'til next spring. What I want you to do is immediate and it could pay very well."

"Could?"

"Look, Mr. Morgan, I've had a very tiring and somewhat frightening day. I don't mind

12

answering your questions, but I would appreciate doing it from the comfort of a chair. I've just come in from a very cold and exhausting one hour walk." Morgan considered her again and then nodded. He took a chair across the room.

"All right, Tammy, let's hear it all."

"My brother and I have inherited some land. We were told it was pretty much worthless and someone made an offer to buy it from us. We were going to accept the offer when we received this message." She'd been fishing through some papers while she talked and now she produced one and handed it to Morgan. He read.

Don't sell. Get help but don't sell.

Morgan looked up. "It doesn't impress the hell out of me, Tammy," he said. "Unsigned and rather poorly written."

"I felt the same way until I turned it over." Morgan frowned and then turned the message over. There was one more line.

Find Lee Morgan. Hire him and then come here.

Morgan looked at Tammy and she was holding out the envelope in which the message had arrived. "Look at the postmark." He did.

"Tombstone, Arizona? Just where in the hell is this land of yours?"

"In California."

"Jeezus! You barge in here, wake me up,

want to hire me to find a killer in Wyoming, tell me it might pay fairly well, and all I have to do is follow you to Arizona on the strength of an unsigned letter to find out about some land you own out in California." Morgan got to his feet. "Tammy, you're crazy."

Tammy stood up also. She had a half smile on her face. "I'm very sure it must look that way but it isn't. My brother will be here in a few minutes and I'll have more answers."

"Like what?"

"Like who wrote this message and, well, maybe why."

"Yeah," Morgan said, "That would be a good start. For all I know there never was a hired man who got himself killed and there is no land and you wrote this."

"Please, Morgan, just bear with me. I swear to you that what I've told you is the truth. You have to believe me." Morgan shook his head. "No, Tammy, that's where you're wrong. I don't have to believe a damned word of it."

"Will you just wait for my brother, please."

Morgan considered her. Actually, he was looking at her for the first time as a woman rather than an intruder. If he had plenty of other doubts, he had none about her womanhood. He snorted and grinned and thought of the messes he seemed to get himself into.

"I'll wait," he said. "The one thing I feel pretty sure about is that you're not going to all this trouble just to rob me." There was just a moment when Tamara Winfrey thought Morgan

14

was serious. Suddenly the tension broke and they both got a big laugh out of it.

Almost on the schedule Tammy had predicted, her brother showed up. He became the second thing about which Morgan was sure. Tad Winfrey was his sister's twin. There was, according to Tammy, just two hours difference between them. Both were twenty-seven. After the appropriate introductions, Tad said, "I've contacted a lawyer friend of mine in Phoenix. We'll know our mystery man soon."

Tad Winfrey was a well groomed, well dressed man who carried no weapons. By Morgan's reckoning, he probably had very little use for them. He was big, husky and, according to him, a skilled pugilist. Morgan knew that boxing wouldn't stop a bullet but it could stop the man with the gun. Tad also proved as long on brains as brawn.

"You know, Mr. Morgan, you've asked a lot of questions of my sister and me. I understand that but I think it's time you answered one, if you can."

"Yeah? What's that?"

"Who do you know in Tombstone, Arizona who would recommend to us that we find you and hire you?"

Morgan couldn't argue the validity of the question. As a matter of fact, he had been somewhat surprised that Tammy hadn't asked it. He was glad she hadn't and was somewhat embarrassed by Tad's having asked. All that aside, it deserved the best answer Morgan could give.

"I don't know a living soul in Tombstone, Arizona," he said. A knock at the door turned all three heads toward it and then glances back at one another. Tad answered. It was the boy from the telegraph office. Tad ripped open the cable and read. He looked up. "My friend used his position as a lawyer to get our answer for us. The sender of the mystery message was Wyatt Earp!"

# 2

Morgan sold his horse. The move was one of simple practicality. It was cheaper to sell him than to transport him. The Winfreys footed the bill for the trip to Tombstone. All but the last leg of it was by rail. They called it an investment but Morgan was quick to point out that he had agreed to nothing more than making the trip.

Morgan reckoned that if Wyatt Earp had actually sent the message, it deserved his attention. If the sender proved to be an imposter, the sender deserved his attention. Either way, in Morgan's view, the long trip was justified.

Enroute, Morgan gave Tad and Tammy the only plausible explanation of which he was aware for the message from Wyatt Earp. Earp, Morgan told them, had been a close friend of

Morgan's father, Buckskin Frank Leslie.

Morgan felt a bit of excitement within himself as the trio walked from the train depot down along the main street toward the Oriental Saloon. At one point along the way, Morgan stopped and stared and pointed to a sign. It read,

O K Corral

"October of eighteen and eighty-one," Morgan said.

Tad Winfrey shook his head and then said, "Sure, I remember reading about the gunfight at the O K Corral." He turned to Morgan. "Was your father in it?"

Morgan shook his head. "I heard that he would have been except for a rainstorm that held up a stagecoach for two days. No, as I remember him telling me, it was the three Earp brothers, Doc Holliday and a gang called the Clanton-McLaury gang."

"Did many die?" Tammy asked.

"Three. Two of the Earp brothers were wounded. Even Doc Holliday got hit, I think, but Wyatt never got a scratch. The other side took the heavy losses."

The three checked into the hotel next to the Oriental and at Morgan's urging got adjacent rooms with a connecting door. Only a few minutes after they were settled in, Morgan knocked.

"You two stay put." He handed Tad a rifle.

Tad frowned. "You know how to use it?"

"I do but. . . ."

"No buts," Morgan said, "not until I find out what's going on. You open the door for me, no one else. If there's more trouble than you can handle," he added, "go through my room and out onto the roof. You can drop from the roof at the far end."

"Are you always this cautious?"

Morgan eyed Tammy and nodded. "Try to remember your hired man."

The Oriental Saloon was jam-packed. Morgan got the eye from one or two of the still unoccupied ladies. One caught his return attention. She was a beautiful octoroon with raven hair pulled into a comb and draped, seductively, over her left shoulder. Morgan made a mental note to inquire about her later.

"What'll you have, mister?" the barkeep asked. Morgan wasn't paying attention and the barkeep repeated the question with a tone of irritation.

"Beer," Morgan said. He was eyeing the back bar and the fancy paintings. There were many tintypes about. The great and near great who had frequented the Oriental over the years. The famed Birdcage Theatre brought them to Tombstone and the Oriental entertained them as they entertained the citizens of Tombstone.

Lily Langtry, Sarah Bernhardt, Georgia Drew and, of course, the famed Little Egypt were among the women. Male entertainers had been equally welcomed however and included the likes of Jack Langrische, Edwin Booth, Maurice Barrymore and the ever popular Eddie Foy.

As Morgan drank his beer, he also considered the infamous who had frequented Tombstone's palaces of pleasure. The Earps, Doc Holliday, John Ringo, Morgan's own father and a score of men Morgan had only read about.

"Another beer, mister?" Morgan blinked, looked up and nodded.

"You look like your father. At least the way he looked when I first knew him." Morgan's head jerked around and he found himself staring into a set of deep blue eyes and a rugged face. The man sported a thick and drooping handlebar moustache, flecked with gray. The skin tone was brown and the texture a bit leathery.

The barkeep returned with Morgan's beer. He took the money and then cast a casual glance at the man who'd moved in next to Morgan. "Evenin', Mr. Earp."

"Charlie."

"I'll be damned," Morgan said. He stood up straight and held out his hand. "You're Wyatt Earp." The man nodded.

"I have a private table in the far corner. Shall we?"

"Sure," Morgan said. Morgan took note of those whose eyes were upon them as they crossed the room. Earp was no doubt one of Tombstone's most colorful characters and he had been one of its first citizens and lawmen. Now the glances carried in them the curiosity of

Morgan's own identity. He was glad when they reached the table.

Morgan had a score of questions. He decided to wet down his throat before he began and took a long swallow of beer. He never got to the questions.

"I sent a message up to Tammy Winfrey. I have to assume she got it and found you. Did all three come with you?"

"Three? Tammy is here and her brother Tad."

Wyatt winced. "Jake Miller?"

"Sorry, never heard of him," Morgan said. Suddenly it dawned on Morgan about the man Tammy said she'd hired. "Tammy told me she had a man working for her. He came looking for me at Fort Laramie. Missed me by a day or two. Got himself killed on the way back to Cheyenne."

Wyatt Earp looked suddenly tired. The sparkle was gone from his eyes and his mouth curled down at the corners. He shook his head back and forth in an almost imperceptible motion. He looked up. "Jake Miller was an old and dear friend. One of the oldtimers in this country. We rode more than one trail together. If Tammy didn't mention him, then he never got to her. It wasn't Jake on that trail but with him dead too, they know about me."

"They? Who the hell is they?" Morgan asked.

Wyatt Earp shook his head again. "The impatience of the young."

"You were never impatient?"

"I was but it's a bad habit for any man who makes his way with a gun."

"I'm not making my way with a gun right now," Morgan said. "I'm trying to get some sensible answers out of somebody, anybody who can give them and when I keep asking and don't get them, I get damned impatient."

"Your father was that way. Impatient as hell, except when he was waiting for a man to make his play. Are you as good as he was?"

"Not from what I've heard. Not from the one time I saw him draw."

"Kid Curry, wasn't it?" Morgan nodded. "I don't think it would have happened that way if Frank Leslie had been your age when he faced Curry." Wyatt scooted his chair back from the table. "I'll be up to see you all tonight, midnight likely, twelve-thirty at the latest." Wyatt Earp got to his feet and it was the first time Morgan noted that the old lawman wasn't carrying a gun.

"You feel safe not toting a piece?"

"Naked is more the word for it," Wyatt said, "but I made a promise to my family. Probably the dumbest promise I ever made and I'll tell you the damned truth, I've never felt comfortable since the day I took it off for good."

"You're not that old," Morgan said, standing up. "And it's obvious you're involved in something here."

"Indirectly is all. I'll tell you about it tonight, Morgan, but I'll tell you this much now.

Tamara and Thaddius are kin to me and I'll not see them hurt. I want the best I can get to help them. In my opinion," Wyatt concluded, smiling, "you're the best around."

"That's a hell of a smooth way to enlist a man's help."

Morgan was surprised to find Wyatt Earp already at the Winfreys' room when he arrived. Wyatt poured Morgan a drink, handed it to him and said, "Morgan, I'd like you to meet these youngsters a second time. This is Tamara and Thaddius Winfrey, the twin children of my sister." Wyatt downed his own shot of whiskey and shook his head a little. "Actually, she was my half sister." He added, quickly, "But I wouldn't have felt any more kinship if she'd have been full blooded Earp."

"Alright," Morgan said, "I'm convinced your request is legitimate. Now how about some of those answers?"

Wyatt nodded, sighed and took a chair. "It could get to sounding like just another frontier tale if I'm not careful, so I'll do my best to keep it simple."

"I'd appreciate that, Wyatt," Morgan said.

"My sister's name was Lileth. She married Holt Winfrey, who could best be described as a dreamer. A prospector with a few more brains than most, but still a dreamer. After about twenty-five years of poking around the rocks trying to find that dream, he did. Big!"

"How big?" Morgan asked.

"Eight to ten million dollars." Morgan's

eyebrows raised and he let go a long, low whistle. Wyatt nodded. "Yes, sir. That's one helluva dream."

"Where'd he hit this Mother Lode?"

"The Palo Verdes range, along the Arroyo Seco at the southeastern tip of California."

Morgan pondered the information for a moment and then looked up and said, "I'm no mining engineer." He grinned, "I wouldn't even qualify as a good prospector but I've never heard of any big strikes in that part of California. What the hell kind of ore was it?"

Wyatt glanced at Tad and Tammy and then back to Morgan. Morgan had caught the glance and now he frowned. Wyatt didn't wait for Morgan to push the issue. "It wasn't ore. It was gold. Pure gold, already mined, already smelted."

"What?"

"Tad," Wyatt said, "maybe you should take it from here."

"My father found the Peralta treasure. I'm sure you've heard of that."

Morgan got up, poured himself another drink, downed it and refilled his glass one more time. Then he turned around and his expression was a mixture of serious doubt and possible anger. "Yeah, I guess damned near everybody who ever rode west of St. Louis, Missouri has heard of the Peralta treasure." Morgan looked down for a moment, obviously in thought. A moment later he looked up, eyed Wyatt and then Tad and Tammy. "I also heard it was bullshit."

Morgan looked at Tammy somewhat sheepishly. "I'm sorry," he said. She smiled and nodded her understanding.

"Tammy's heard a lot worse," Tad said, "from me. I didn't believe it either and I know there must be a thousand legends about buried Spanish gold."

"If you know that, Tad," Morgan said, pouring himself another drink, "then you also know that not so much as one twenty dollar gold piece has been found."

"Yes, I know that, too, but this is different."

"Sounds that way, if he actually found gold. Have you seen it?"

"He didn't find the gold, I mean, not the gold itself." Morgan laughed. Tad's face flushed with the first hint of anger. Morgan downed his drink and looked at Wyatt. Morgan was rather hoping for some support from the old lawman. Wyatt's expression didn't indicate that he was about to give in.

"What the hell did he find, Tad? A damned map?"

Wyatt Earp said, "Do me the favor of hearing the story, Morgan. I'm no damned fool for Spanish gold. I listened and I changed my mind."

"I'm here," Morgan replied, coldly, "and my expenses are paid. Listening to another treasure story seems little enough to do to earn my keep." Morgan sat down, crossed his legs, folded his arms across his chest and said, "Go ahead, Tad, I'm listening."

"I promise I won't bore you with another Spanish gold legend."

Morgan admired Tad's spunk but he really didn't want to hear another tale of buried treasure. "I'll hold you to that," Morgan said.

"Simply put," Tad began, "Francisco Peralta rode into California seeking land, not gold. He stumbled into an Indian village in which the tribe used gold for virtually everything. Their tools, dishes, replicas of their Gods. Peralta got the fever. He wiped out the village and then spent six months rounding up wild horses and breaking them for pack animals."

"And what went wrong?"

"The usual. Internal at first. Men who weren't content with a bonus in their pay. They wanted a share. The longer it went, the more they became unhappy. Only a raid on the Spanish camp by Mexican bandits unified them again."

"And the gold?"

"Still with them but Peralta knew he'd never get it back to Spain. Besides, by that time he was already considering some pretty horrible alternatives."

"Like keeping it all for himself?" Morgan smiled. He'd heard it all before. Different names and places but the same story.

Tad knew that Morgan didn't buy any of the story. It angered him somewhat, but he tried to remember that, at first, neither had Wyatt Earp. He ignored Morgan's question and just continued. "Peralta ordered eighty percent of the gold loaded onto the newly broken horses. Twenty percent he loaded onto the expedition's pack mules, then he split the two groups. The smaller of the two carried the most wealth.''

''And the other one was a decoy, a sacrificial lamb he sent to the slaughter.''

''Exactly.''

Morgan smiled again. It was like reading an old newspaper. ''Did it work?''

''It did. The smaller force was attacked and wiped out. It gave Peralta enough time to reach the mountains.''

''The Palo Verdes.''

''No. A range to the south which, at that time, didn't have a name. Today it's called the Cargo Muchacho range. The mountains of the remorseful boy.'' Morgan cocked his head. Tad went on. ''There were about two hundred boys riding with Peralta. They were the newest conscripts into the army and he'd asked permission to take them on the five year trip so that they might return home as men. Among them was his own grandson.''

''That's all he had with him in the main body? Boys?''

''No. There was still a contingent of troops under an officer who completely trusted Peralta. The Spaniard had chosen a plan and now set it in motion. He sent the captain and the rest of the soldiers south, ordering them to find a passable route through the mountains and into Mexico.

''But they didn't find it and Peralta, stuck with a pack of rug rats, had to bury the gold.''

Tad was becoming increasingly irritated by Morgan's chiding. He looked to Wyatt for support but the old lawman just smiled. Tad turned back, his jaw set, his eyes piercing.

"No, Morgan, they didn't find it. What they found were Indians and Mexican bandits and death. It was exactly what Peralta had hoped they'd find."

Morgan frowned. "You saying he planned it that way?"

"That's what I'm saying, yes. You see, almost the instant the soldiers rode out, Peralta ordered the boys into groups of about fifty each. Four of them. They divided up the gold and over the next four days, rode in four directions and buried it. Peralta's grandson accompanied each of the four groups and made a drawing of the burial spot. By the time the last group had returned, Peralta had the only map depicting all four areas. No one else, not even his grandson, knew all four locations."

"I'll be damned," Morgan said, "now that's a new one."

"Yes, Morgan, it is, so to speak, a new one and not the only new one where the Peralta gold is concerned."

"I'm listening."

Tad smiled. For the first time, he believed Morgan really was listening. "The soldiers had not returned. If the captain had been easily persuaded by Peralta's manner, you can imagine how he handled the boys."

"He ordered them into the field?"

"Not only that, he split them up again. Groups of fifty in four directions. This time, they were told not to stop until they found a way out."

"Jeezus! How many made it?"

"There are no records that any of them made it. If they did, they were too damned scared to ride back or try to tell their story to anyone."

"Peralta?"

Tad held up his hands. "I'll get to that." He walked across the room, warming now to a subject he'd obviously researched very thoroughly. "Peralta had kept two other people behind when he ordered the last contingent of troops away. One was the priest. The other, a metalsmith."

"The priest for the boys, the metalsmith to melt the stuff down into," Morgan paused, "into what? Coins? Bricks?"

"You're right about the priest, Morgan. Not to have kept him back with the boys would have aroused too much suspicion. The metalsmith is another story."

"I'm still listening."

"Peralta's wife had presented him with a brand new brace of pistols before he left. Pistols with wooden butts. Now, Peralta ordered the metalsmith to fashion new grips for them. Grips of gold, each of which would depict a portion of the four burial sites of the treasure. Only someone with both pistols would have the complete map. As each grip was completed,

29

Peralta destroyed the accompanying map made by his grandson."

"And he'd have to destroy the metalsmith and the priest too."

"Exactly," Tad said.

"And Peralta? Did he make it?"

"Only one person rode out of that mountain range, Morgan."

"The grandson! What the hell happened?"

"That we don't know for sure. Maybe no one ever will."

"The kid didn't get the gold either," Morgan said, "and that's the remorse."

"If the grandson followed in his grandfather's footsteps, yes. But there was plenty to be remorseful about without the gold. The boy's grandfather was dead, the soldiers were dead, his friends were dead. He was twelve, maybe fifteen. He was all alone."

"Well," Morgan said, walking over to the whiskey bottle again, "it's one of the best gold stories I've heard." He poured a little shorter shot and downed it and then turned to face the trio. He smiled. "I'll give it that." None of them smiled back.

Tad Winfrey crossed the room to a chair in the far corner. Draped over its back was a set of saddlebags. Tad stepped into Morgan's line of sight, removed something from one of the bags and turned around. Morgan stared. His smile faded. He was looking at the rusty frame of an old flintlock pistol. A pistol with a gold grip.

# 3

Morgan slept on what he'd heard and seen and there were plenty of questions to which he wanted answers but he'd decided to throw in with Wyatt Earp. He'd agreed to meet Wyatt the next morning and he assumed Wyatt would want an answer. He was wrong.

At ten o'clock, Morgan strolled into the Arizona Bank & Trust Company and soon found himself in company with Wyatt and the bank's president, John Hemmings. After the introductions, Morgan got his biggest surprise yet.

"Read this," Wyatt said, handing Morgan what appeared to be an official document. Morgan read. His expression hardened as he read and when he finished he tossed the paper on the desk.

"You mind if we talk privately for a moment, Mr. Hemmings? Morgan was looking at Wyatt Earp the whole time he was speaking. It was Wyatt who responded.

"I'm sure he wouldn't mind Morgan, but there's no need. He's involved in this thing a helluva lot deeper than I am right now." Wyatt leaned forward, "Mr. Hemmings here is puttin' up the money and I won't let 'im do that unless the man that I recommend for the job is wearin' a badge."

"I don't much like wearing badges, Wyatt."

"And I don't much like hired gun hands, Morgan, which is exactly what you'd be without the badge. Take it or leave it."

Morgan had an odd sense of obligation, somehow, and he resented it. Wyatt Earp had been almost as much a legend to him as the Peralta treasure, until now. He eyed both men.

"I don't like the idea of justifying hiring out my gun by pinning on a tin star."

Wyatt leaned back and smiled. "Then don't justify it, I don't give a damn and I'm sure Mr. Hemmings doesn't either. But without the badge, you can catch the afternoon stage back north. You got expenses for both directions."

"Why did you wait 'til this morning to spring this on me?"

"Because if you didn't believe the rest of it, there was no need for this morning."

"Who says I do believe it?"

"You showed up."

Morgan leaned forward. "I showed up because you're Wyatt Earp, not necessarily because I believe that gold legend or a rusty old pistol with a shiny grip."

"Then sign that paper for the same reason, Morgan, and do us both a favor." Wyatt reached into his vest pocket and pulled out a small cloth sack. He said, "You know, if you come out o' this in one piece, you could be a wealthy man." He put the sack on the desk in front of Morgan. Morgan eyed it.

"When I sit in a poker game," Morgan said, "I like to know ever'body who's going to play."

"When you're ready to play," Wyatt Earp countered, "I'll be glad to tell you as much as I know." He pointed at the cloth sack. Morgan picked it up, undid the draw strings and let the contents spill into his hand. It was a badge. A shiny brass badge.

### United States Marshal

"Real pretty," Morgan said.

"It was given to me by John Fremont when he appointed me marshal right here in Tombstone back in the summer of eighty. I only wore it once," Wyatt said, "had a silver one for ever-'day."

"Go to meeting badge, was it?" Morgan asked.

"I'd reckon that's what Fremont had in mind, but I didn't wear it for that. I wore it on the twenty-sixth day of October, eighteen and eighty-one."

Morgan's eyes widened. "The shootout at the O K corral?"

Wyatt nodded. "Put it on that mornin' and left it on 'til they'd buried Tom and Frank McLaury and Billy Clanton. Never pinned it on again. I'd like you to wear it." Wyatt had a carpetbag next to him and he opened it and handed Morgan a Buntline Special.

"I've heard about this gun, but this is the first one I ever saw."

"More'n likely be the last, too," Wyatt said. "The folks up to Colt don't figure on makin' any more of 'em. Now, Morgan, I want that badge back." Morgan looked up. Wyatt was smiling. "No hole in it, neither." He nodded toward the long barreled pistol. "That gun is yours to keep, whether you ride in this thing or not." Morgan looked puzzled. "I owed your daddy." Wyatt paused in obvious remembrance. "Helluva man, your daddy. Sometime I'll tell you about the marker he held on me. In the meanwhile, I'd like you to accept the gun for him."

Morgan looked up. He knew Wyatt Earp was not a man to offer a bribe to get what he wanted and he was thinking to himself exactly what Buckskin Frank Leslie would be saying to him. He'd have told Morgan to ride for Wyatt just because Earp asked him to, no other reason necessary, no questions asked.

Lee Morgan had become his own man, no question about that, but he was now being exposed to a part of his heritage which was becoming almost as scarce as buffalo herds. The code, his father called it. The unwritten, unspoken tie which linked certain men together. There were times and places for questions and for caution and for saying no. Morgan remembered what his father had said. "You don't say no to a friend. That's the code."

"You've got yourself a gun," Morgan said.

Wyatt Earp smiled. "I could have got a gun in a half a dozen places, Morgan. It's the man behind it I was picky about." He extended his hand and Morgan gripped it firmly. He'd ridden many trails for many reasons, but he'd never ridden one for the code. It was time he did.

Lee Morgan learned another quick lesson about the code. It was one lonely sonuvabitch! The Winfreys had their own set of duties to perform and would be making the trip to California nearly two weeks after Morgan was already there. As to Wyatt Earp, he had a family and a promise to them and home. He went back to it.

Morgan received five hundred dollars in expenses from the banker, Wyatt standing good for it, and a letter of credit for any additional funds he might need. His destination was the little desert town which Holt Winfrey put together after he'd made his discovery.

Morgan rode through a pass in the Cargo Muchacho range and down into the God forsaken desert below it. It was land on which, Morgan reckoned, a man couldn't raise hell with a fifth of whiskey. Holtville, California, offered little in the way of respite from it.

Morgan bought himself a new wardrobe in Tombstone and it included a fine cowhide vest. Beneath it, pinned on his left shirt pocket, he wore the marshal's badge. He decided he'd likely end up a target for somebody before this trail ended but he didn't intend to make it easy for them.

The Holtville Hotel had some things in common with some of the finest establishments in the country. A front door, at least one window in each room, and a chamber pot. If there were other similarities, Morgan was damned if he could find them.

"How long will you be with us, sir?"

"Not sure," Morgan said, "looking to buy some land hereabouts and there seems to be plenty of it to see. Could be quite a spell." The desk clerk was giving Morgan the once-over all the time Morgan was talking. He took particular note of Morgan's rig and the extra special rig which Morgan now wore in a cross drawn fashion on his left hip. It was Wyatt's Buntline Special.

"You, uh, well, you don't look the cut of a land buyer." The clerk looked at the registration book and frowned. The name meant nothing to him. Morgan picked up his gear. He looked the clerk right in the eye.

"Funny," he said, "you don't look like a desk clerk."

Morgan settled in and then took a turn around the town. It wasn't much. He reckoned that it had been at one time and he was certain that Holt Winfrey had good intentions. The town just didn't match the dream. A third of the buildings along the main street were boarded up. There were half a dozen run-down saloons, a drug store, a mercantile, a tonsorial parlor, one eatery which boasted home cooked meals, a law office, the Holtville Bank and the sheriff's office.

Morgan's tour was kept to the main street, although he got a glimpse of a railroad depot and one or two rather large and pretentious looking homes on a tree-lined side street. He promised himself a more thorough tour later.

The door to his room was ajar and Morgan tensed up. He approached cautiously and he could hear voices.

"You check that carpetbag?"

"Not yet. Nothin' important in these saddle bags, though."

"Looks like our visitin' land buyer just bought himself some new clothes. Don't appear these duds been wore yet."

There was a loose and squeaky floor board just outside Morgan's room. By whatever chance applies, he'd missed stepping on it when he checked in. Now, he found it.

"Shit," he mumbled, looking down. The door flew open and Morgan didn't see the meaty fist coming. It connected.

Morgan reeled backwards, slammed into the wall across the narrow hall and found the wind half knocked out of him. He shook his head and brought his arms up to defend himself. It was already too late. The man who'd hit him was built like a battering ram. Short and stocky and solid and with a head like a boulder. He doubled up and put the boulder right into Morgan's middle. The gunman folded up over the man's muscular shoulders. He lifted Morgan, spun around and literally tossed Morgan through the door to his own room. He felt his arms being pinned behind him by the second man and he could see the battering ram coming at him again. It was the last thing he saw for some little time.

What Morgan saw an hour later seemed to be floating. He blinked and some things looked more solid. He drew a breath and moaned. A moment later, a bearded face came into view as Morgan pushed himself up on his elbows. He blinked again and the last of the blur disappeared, replaced by a clear vision of iron bars.

"Glad to see you're still with us, Marshal. I've seen more'n one gent stove up for a month or more after tanglin' with Shorty." Morgan got to his feet. Instinctively he felt for his gun. "Got your hardware out here, Marshal." The man pulled the cell door open. Obviously, it hadn't been locked.

Morgan noted that there were only two cells, with no one using either but him. The bearded man had already gone into the small office at the building's front. Morgan now followed. The bearded man was gathering up Morgan's guns. He turned around just as Morgan's eyes fell on Shorty. The bearded man grinned.

"I'm Sheriff Prather," he said, stepping

quickly in between Morgan and Shorty. He handed Morgan his six-gun and the empty holster in which Morgan had been carrying the long barreled Buntline. Morgan frowned. "Got that fancy pistol in muh desk drawer there. Didn't want to chance anybody stealin' it." The sheriff wiped his hand on the seat of his pants and then extended it. "Tyson Prather. Most call me Ty," he said, and then added, "when they git to know me."

Morgan declined the handshake and strapped on his rig instead. The sheriff stepped aside, gestured toward Shorty with his left hand and said, "I think you two already met but I'll introduce ya jist the same. This here is one o' muh deputies, Shorty. T'other one's eatin' his supper. Name's Luther." He motioned for Shorty to stand up. The deputy did, grinning the whole time. "Shorty, this gent here is a honest to God Yewnited States Marshal name o' Lee Morgan." Ty Prather turned back to face Morgan. "Shorty, he never met no real marshal before."

"You've got a lousy welcoming committee in your town," Morgan said, stepping by the sheriff and moving to the desk. He opened the top drawer, glanced down, slammed it shut, and opened a side drawer. In it was the Buntline. He took it out and slipped it into the holster. He looked up. Ty Prather was frowning at Morgan's audacity but Shorty was scowling.

"We don't git too many strangers in Holt-ville, Mr. Morgan, and I can't recollect the last time we had a visit from a Yewnited States Marshal. As the duly elected lawman in town, it's muh duty to find out a stranger's name an' intent."

"Did you ever hear of asking questions?"

Sheriff Prather shuffled his feet, looked down and then ran his fingers through dirty looking, stringy hair and said, "Well, sir, now I just got to apologize fer that there. Ya see, I was out o' town on important business an' Shorty here, he kind o' takes the job too serious sometimes." Prather looked up. "I'd likely do more to both of 'em, Marshal, but them bein' named Prather too," he grinned, "well sir, you can see muh problem. Them bein' kin an' all."

"Yeah, Sheriff," Morgan said, "I understand." He came from behind the desk and walked straight over to the two men. "Now you understand something. I'm going to be with you for a spell and I'm here officially. I hope nobody gets in my way."

Morgan saw Ty Prather's hand move backwards and still a threatened move by Shorty. Morgan had been ready but there was no need to stir more trouble than he'd already encountered.

"As one lawman to another, Mr. Morgan, I sure would feel better if we could work together, yessir. An' I'll see to it nobody gits in your way. You can count on me, Marshal, sure enough you can."

Morgan said nothing else and didn't bother acknowledging Ty Prather's commitment. He wasn't certain just exactly how the brothers

Prather had managed the only badges in town, but he was certain it wasn't by the Democratic process. He vowed to find out and to be a helluva lot more careful in the days to come.

Behind him, in the office of Sheriff Ty Prather, the grimy looking lawman picked up his hat and used it to flog his brother about the head and shoulders.

"Goddam it, Shorty, I tol' you a hunnert times, if'n I tol' you once, you don't do nuthin' less'n you ask me first." He flogged some more and only the arrival of Luther, or Lutey as he was known generally, stopped the flogging. Ty proceeded to administer a like punishment to Lutey and then said, "Shorty, now you ride on out to the ranch an' you tell Judge Lunsford what we found an' what we got. You hear?"

"How's come I got to go? Lutey eat his supper, I ain't."

Ty Prather let go another barrage with his hat. "You go 'cause I said you go. If I wanted Lutey to go, I'd send Lutey."

Morgan found himself some supper and more sore stomach muscles than he'd first believed and a lot of curious citizens. He ate and departed as quickly as his digestion would allow. He did want to make one more stop before he returned to his room. He found the off duty desk clerk playing poker. The clerk sensed Morgan's presence next to him and looked up. He looked puzzled.

"If you pass out anymore keys to my room, you and I will meet again and it won't be to talk.

41

You understand me?" The man sitting next to the clerk stiffened. He was a burly man with a thick neck and a face scarred from a bout with the pox.

"You make threats against my friends, mister, you make threats against me." The man pushed back from the table and the clerk smiled. The man got up. Morgan was in no mood to get caught off guard and let somebody else get in the first lick. As a matter of fact, at that moment, he was not even in the mood for a good old, one on one, fair fight barroom brawl.

"Mister," Morgan said, calmly, "I'm not talking to you." He drew the Buntline and laid the barrel across the man's head.

Morgan washed down with the coolest water he could find and stretched out, shirtless, on his bed. He was dozing in a few minutes, but his right hand was firm around the butt of the Bisley Colts. The squeaky hallway floor board worked again. This time to Morgan's advantage.

His eyes opened, fast and wide. He moved quietly but quickly off the bed. The door was locked and he fixed his gaze to the knob. It turned once, then again. Morgan waited. The floorboard squeaked and Morgan made his move.

He was at the door, had it unlocked and wide open in almost one fluid move. The door opened in and to the right of someone on the inside. He flung it open and stepped left. He heard footsteps pick up speed. He peered cautiously to his right and then wheeled into the hallway in a crouch, Bisley at the ready.

"That's far enough, unless you want a walking stick for a spell." The intruder stopped. "Turn around." The intruder complied. "Jeezus!" The intruder proved to be a kid, twelve to fifteen years old, Morgan reckoned. He stood up and motioned for the kid to come to him. Still, he kept the Bisley aimed at him.

*"Buenas noches, señor* Morgan."

"Good evening hell! *"No habla Ingles."*

The boy shrugged. *"No habla Ingles."*

Morgan stuffed the Bisley into his waistband. He thought a moment. *"Como te llamas?"*

*"Me llamo* Felipe."

It had been sometime since Morgan had to test his Spanish. He paused again and then said, *"En que' puedo servirle?"*

"He came for me, *señor."* Morgan looked up toward the end of the hall. The girl he saw standing there was one of the most beautiful he'd ever seen. Clearly she was Spanish but she had breeding. The inky black hair was swept up and held in place with combs. Most of it, Morgan reckoned, was hidden beneath the flat, black hat. She wore leather britches, a white silk blouse and a short leather vest atop it. The britches were molded to shapely hips and thighs and Morgan could see the considerable stress on the silk blouse.

"Why?" Morgan asked.

"I knew you would not kill a boy."

Morgan smirked. "That right." She nodded. "But you didn't figure I'd have any trouble

43

gunning down a woman."

"I didn't mean that," she said. Just then, the boy bolted away and hurried to her. Morgan eyed them both. "He is my brother."

"Damned dangerous thing to do, lady, sending in a kid."

"I was," she hesitated, and then sighed, "I was wrong."

"Uh huh, you were but now that you're here, you may as well come in."

"I will send Felipe home first."

"I wouldn't. I've had other visitors since I hit town and they weren't quite as friendly with their approach."

In Morgan's room the woman and the boy stood in the corner huddled together. They both looked scared but Morgan could see a look of determination in the woman's eyes. He'd seen the look before. The look of a woman who'd been wronged or scorned. He remembered something about the wrath of a woman scorned. He also knew it applied to a woman wronged.

"You said someone visited you earlier. May I ask who?"

"Your friendly local deputies."

"They are evil men. They enforce only one law."

"Their own?"

"That of Don Miguel Carbona."

Morgan's ears picked up. It was a name he recognized and he didn't know why.

"Carbona? It's familiar to me." He considered the woman. "Any idea why it should be?"

"Perhaps you read of him, *señor*. He was charged with financing a raid on the Mexican border town of Tecolote."

"Yeah," Morgan said, nodding, "I remember now but they acquitted him, didn't they?"

The woman smirked. "Of course they did. Would it be otherwise when his best friend is Josiah Lunsford?" It was another name which struck a familiar chord. Morgan came up with that reason on his own.

"I saw that name on one or two of the stores in town."

"More than that, *señor*, but his main business is what saved Don Miguel."

"And what would that be?"

"He is the Federal Judge."

Morgan pondered the names and the obvious power which they had behind them and began to wonder just what the hell he was into.

"Seems to me it's time to talk about you, lady. Who you are and why you're here."

"I was told to contact you when you arrived. I had to make certain you were the right man. There is much at stake, *señor* Morgan."

"Who told you to contact me?"

"I cannot say that now but I know you are Lee Morgan, and I know you are a U.S. Marshal."

"And who the hell are you?"

The woman took a deep breath and said, "Estralita Peralta."

45

# 4

Morgan found sleep elusive following the woman's revelation. Neither the Winfreys or Wyatt Earp had bothered to tell him there were Peraltas still around. He wondered if, in fact, they themselves knew it. He was up and down a half a dozen times and it was well after two o'clock in the morning before he finally dozed off.

The shotgun blast tore a hole in the room's door big enough for a man's head to pass through. The second blast ripped into the center of the bed and showered Morgan in a blizzard of ticking. The gunman had already vacated the bed even before the first blast, however, and now it was Morgan and not his assailant who had the edge.

Morgan had rolled from the bed with the

first sounds in the hallway. He picked the side nearest the door and then pressed his back to the wall nearest the door. After a second blast, Morgan jerked open the door, spinning into position at the same time. He fired two shots and two men died.

He'd fully expected to see the two seedy deputies, but neither of the men in the hallway were men he'd seen before. Moments later however, the deputies did arrive. One at each end of the hallway. Shorty approached Morgan while the one called Lutey stood by with a shotgun. Morgan eyed them both.

"Lawman or no lawman, mister," Shorty said, grinning, "we don't tolerate no gunplay in Holtville."

"There was no play to it," Morgan said, "these two tried to leave their brand on me with shotguns."

"That so? Well now, mister fancy ass Marshal, we'll jist let the judge decide that. We got a good 'un here, ya know."

Morgan remembered Estralita Peralta's description of the good judge. A Federal Judge, no less. Lunsford, Morgan recalled. He also remembered that the Federal Territorial Prison was too damned close for comfort. The worst Federal Prison in the country was at Yuman, Airzona.

Morgan shrugged and dropped his pistol. At the same time he glanced down the hall toward Lutey. "Oh shit," he screamed, pointing at the same time. Lutey was predictable. He whirled around. By then, Shorty was about five feet from Morgan. The gunman would have liked nothing better than to take Shorty out back and beat the piss out of him but there simply wasn't time.

Morgan telegraphed his right leg with deadly accuracy. He wished he had his boots on but the ball of his foot found the target, Shorty's balls. Morgan expected Shorty to bend forward. He did and Morgan's knee greeted him on the chin.

Shorty went down like a poled ox and Morgan vanished into his room. By then Lutey knew he'd been sharked and when he saw Shorty, he bellowed at the top of his lungs and came charging down the hall. Morgan couldn't afford to kill a deputy sheriff and the man was brandishing a sawed-off.

Morgan grabbed his bedroll and freed up the black snake whip. He had it uncoiled just as Lutey reached the door. By then Lutey's brain was working and he stopped short of coming into view.

"Shorty. Shit! Goddam! You kilt 'im, ya sonuvabitch. You'll hang fer this, sure."

"You've got me," Morgan said. He tossed his pistol into the hallway. Lutey displayed a sudden show of smarts which Morgan wouldn't have imagined he possessed.

"You ain't foolin' me none, Marshal," he said, "you still got the long barreled pistol." Morgan smiled and shook his head. He slipped the Buntline from its holster and tossed it into the hallway as well.

"You're too smart for me, deputy." The compliment now also took effect and turned Lutey's brain back to mush. He stepped into view and Morgan unleashed the black snake. The shotgun flew into the air as the whip's end wrapped itself around Lutey's right wrist. Morgan worked the whip again.

Lutey was howling at the top of his lungs and holding his wrist. He didn't even see the second attack. Morgan aimed low and put two coils around Lutey's legs just below the knees. Morgan pulled and Lutey Prather ended up on his ass. Morgan walked himself along the whip, freed Lutey's legs and then pressed Lutey's own shotgun against the deputy's belly.

"I've got some questions, Deputy, and as long as I keep getting answers, this shotgun won't go off." Lutey stopped howling and he was scared, but brother Ty had trained him well.

"You won't shoot no lawman. You're one yourself." He forced a half smile. Morgan half straightened up, gave Lutey a weak smile in return, shrugged, turned the shotgun end for end and swung the butt in a short arc. The end of it caught Lutey on the chin and the obese little deputy joined Shorty in a heap.

Morgan didn't wait for morning. He gathered his gear and slipped out a side entrance. The man at the livery emerged from his quarters in long johns, bleary eyed and toting an old single shell shotgun. Morgan simply flashed the brass badge and the man returned to his quarters without a word. Morgan rode out, headed east. He was supposed to meet Estralita Peralta and he'd decided he wanted to be at their meeting place ahead of her.

The sand hills were strung out for two hundred miles in a diagonal pattern which ran from northwest to southeast. It was country in which a man could easily lose his way, either by accident or design. The wind was perpetual and made short work of tracks. Morgan had agreed to a meeting place with which he was already familiar. There were four roads through the sand hills. They converged at one point and Morgan had been there when he rode into the country.

As he sat and waited for the Peralta woman, he grew more and more uneasy. His mind was reeling with unanswered questions and each passing day brought new threats, new faces, more questions and no goddamn answers. The Winfreys and even Wyatt Earp had been of no help in that sense. They gave him information and directions and legends but no answers.

Morgan's horse snorted and pawed the ground. Morgan looked up and the animal had turned and was looking toward a nearby rise to the southeast. Morgan levered a shell into the Winchester and got to his feet. The horse snorted again and turned its head to the right. So did Morgan, then back to the left and then straight ahead.

"Jeezus!" The entire crest of the ridge of sand which overlooked the road junction was covered with riders. Morgan could only guess how many, and he did, in his mind. A hundred, he guessed.

Lee Morgan had been potato-sacked over a saddle only one other time in his life. He'd been scouting for the Army and found himself the unwilling guest of a Sioux war party. Now, he was the equally unwilling guest of a small army of Mexican banditos. Making matters worse was a blindfold and a gag and some damned sore ribs from his first meeting with Shorty.

Morgan estimated an hour on the animal from the road junction to the camp where they eventually ended up. He was untied. Then his captors trussed him up with his wrists bound to his ankles, his arms pulled behind him. He was dumped finally and only then did he lose the blindfold and the gag. He saw no one. He found himself in what he reckoned was a two-man Army field tent.

The day wore on, the sun grew hot, the thirst great and still Morgan saw no one. He kept conjuring up a vision of that beautiful face in the hallway. Estralita Peralta had considered the possibility that Morgan might gun her. Right at that moment, he thought, it would not only be easy but it might be pleasurable.

Morgan did his best to roll and find a new position and a little more comfort. Too, he knew he mustn't let the blood circulation get too low in his legs. His eyes got big.

The scorpion was on his leg, just above the knees and working its way up. Another was crawling along the sand about four feet away, headed straight for Morgan's face. He didn't move and he was wondering if scorpions had ears. If he shouted, would they hear him too? The tent flap opened and Morgan was momentarily blinded by the brightness.

"Don't move, for Chrissakes," he said, "I've got two scorpions on me."

"I know," came the reply, "I turned them into the tent to see if you'd scream. Most men do." A moment later the insects were dead in the sand and Morgan's wrists were free of his ankles. The girl was on her knees next to him, smiling. "Would you have screamed?"

"Why the hell didn't you wait it out and see?"

She smiled. "I would have, Mr. Morgan, but you would have been stung and died and there are others here who seem to think you have very valuable information."

"But you don't agree?"

"That's right. Now, can you sit up by yourself or do you want some help?"

"Why the hell don't you cut me loose? If that little army I saw is outside, I'm sure as hell not going anywhere." The girl ignored him. "Do you want help or not?" He nodded.

The girl looked vaguely familiar but she was not the girl in the hallway. She was not Estralita Peralta. She got Morgan to a sitting position. In spite of everything, Morgan could not ignore the girl's body or her soft touch or a faint feminine odor which stirred something deep within him. He had a need which had not been fulfilled for too long.

"I can tell you, lady," Morgan said, "you're right and your friends are wrong. I don't know a damned thing that will be of any use to them."

She smiled. "And even if you do, Marshal, you're the kind of man who would die before you'd reveal it."

"Your percentage just went down, lady," Morgan said, "on that one, you're wrong."

"I don't believe you, Mr. Morgan, but I can assure you of one thing," she said, turning around, "we will both have ample opportunity to put it to the test." She crawled out of the tent.

"How about some water?" Morgan hollered. There was no reply. He began at once to test the strength of his bonds. He cursed under his breath. These were not amateurs. The bonds were leather and short of his Bowie knife, or someone else's, they would not be removed. "Spanish fucking gold," he muttered. "Nice move, Morgan, real nice move."

Morgan's next visitor, perhaps an hour later, was no shapely, attractive, sweetly scented female. Morgan was yanked from the tent by his hair and found a boot resting on the side of his neck while a second man cut his bonds. Slowly, Morgan got to his feet. He'd barely done so when the big Mexican rammed a rifle butt into his soler plexus. Morgan's knees, already tingling from the bonds so lately removed, buckled.

"You stay on your feet Yankee dog, in the presence of our leader." Morgan was pulled back to his feet, his arms were pinned behind him and the second man struck three solid blows. Morgan went down again when he was turned loose. He shook his head and gulped in air. He tensed his muscles and struggled to his hands and knees. He could see a leg being drawn back.

"That's enough, Paco. He's no good to us dead." The voice was feminine and Morgan recognized it as that of the girl he knew as Estralita Peralta. A few minutes later, he found himself in a large tent attached to a make shift lean-to. He was pushed into a chair. He sat facing a big, muscular man whose dress was most definitely that of a Mexican bandit. What happened next surprised Morgan even in his condition.

"I'm certain you expected to be dragged before some kind of animal with a name like El Lobo or El Diablo."

Morgan eyed the man. He was dressed in typical Mexican attire and the trappings matched. A silver band around the base of the crown of his hat, silver encrusted, crossed bandoliers, twin, ivory gripped pistols, twin, bone handled Bowie knives and a bolo knife in a shoulder sheath. Its grip protruded above the man's left shoulder.

"You sure as hell look like one or the other," Morgan said. The man smiled. He turned to the girl and said, "Get Mr. Morgan some water." She nodded. He turned back to face Morgan. "Later some tequila or even wine perhaps." Morgan said nothing until he had consumed two large cups of water. He asked for a third and dumped it over his head.

"If you worked for me, I'd have you shot for what you just did."

Morgan mopped the water out of his eyes and face and then looked up and said, "If I worked for you, I'd have done it a long time back."

The man smiled. "You are a man who makes hasty judgments. You don't know me and you don't know what I do or why I do it, yet you have already acquired a dislike for me."

"That's a powerful bit of understatement," Morgan shot back.

"Then let me give you some information."

"Why not just give me back my belongings and my horse instead?"

"I'm afraid that's quite impossible. I'm surprised you'd even bother to ask."

"My daddy used to say you never know unless you ask."

"Frank Leslie, wasn't he?" Morgan was surprised. He showed it. He nodded.

"I know a great deal about you, Mr. Morgan, and now I propose to tell you a little about myself. My name is not El Lobo or El Diablo. I am not the Mexican bandito or the comanchero you would read about in the American press or the dime novels. My name is Joaquin Francisco Marin." Estralita brought Marin a flask. He opened it and took a short pull. He released it, handed it back to her and said, "Medicinal only."

"Get to the point, Marin."

The man cocked his head. "Very well. Let me

spell it out for you. My family was Spanish, not Mexican, not at the beginning in any event. The gold which was, shall I say, confiscated by *señor* Peralta belonged to my family. It was Marin money which financed the expedition, not Peralta's."

"Uh huh. So you've come up from Spain to claim your rightful heritage. Just a nice, neighborly fellow riding at the head of a gang of gun slinging, knife toting cutthroats."

"There is somewhat more to it than that, but you don't seem interested in hearing the truth or the details."

"The truth? I've met damned few people in the last few weeks who know the meaning of the word and none of them live within a day's ride of here. Just what the hell do you want from me, Marin?"

"The pistol with the gold grip. Don't bother denying your knowledge of it. Now you either have it or you know who does and therefore have access to it. I want it and I have a deadline. Produce it and you save your life."

"And you're going to take my word for what I tell you, let me ride out of here and get it and bring it back, that right?"

Marin smiled and shook his head. "You Americans and your sense of humor. It has seen you through many ordeals, hasn't it?" Morgan didn't reply. "Of course, you will simply tell me what I need to know. Your own life is the best security for both of us. If my men return with the pistol, you go free. If they do not, I'll have you killed." Marin got to his feet, held up his hand at a point when it appeared Morgan was about to speak. "I want you to think about it. Think about it very carefully," he paused, "until tomorrow."

"I do have one question Marin, before tomorrow." Marin stopped and turned back. "Why the hell is a girl named Peralta in your camp?"

Marin cocked his head and shrugged. "A lie, sir. I wasn't certain what you knew or did not know. I was sure of only one thing. You would meet a Peralta, not a Marin."

Morgan didn't have to wait long before he found himself once again in company with the two Mexicans. This time, however, he was also joined by Estralita Peralta, or whoever the hell she was.

"There is no need to bind him, Paco." Morgan had steeled himself to resist being tied up again. He hadn't the vaguest idea what he intended to do after he won the fight with Paco, if indeed he won the fight with Paco, but the consideration became academic. "You will ride with us to the house," she said. Morgan didn't say anything but he was wondering where the hell this house was located. He soon found out.

It was Spanish architecture at its finest. A tree-lined, green oasis in the middle of nowhere and with more security, Morgan reckoned, than Yuma prison could boast.

Morgan was given an upstairs room with an adjacent water closet and sunken bath. He was in need of both and ignored the barred windows and half a hundred armed guards.

Morgan's eyes were closed and he let the warm water soak into his bruised, aching muscles. Escape, deals, gold, the Winfreys, even Wyatt Earp could not rouse him now. He was dead ass tired and if he died tomorrow he intended to enjoy today.

He heard the movement behind him so he wasn't being careless. He just didn't give a damn.

"Wine?" He nodded. He heard the liquid being poured, a soft hand touched his arm. He put the glass to his lips and savored the taste. It was good wine and cool on his parched lips and throat. He still hadn't opened his eyes. Now, the same soft hands became more firm in their touch. Fingers dug in and worked on taut shoulder and back muscles.

"That's good," Morgan said.

"What? The wine or the massage?"

"Both and I'll take more of both." Morgan thought that Wyatt Earp would tell him he was fraternizing with the enemy. "Go to hell, Earp."

"What?" Morgan took a second glass of wine, smiled and opened his eyes. "Who did you say?"

"Nothing," Morgan replied, "forget it." He looked up. It was the girl who called herself Estralita. "What's your real name?"

"Teresa Marin. The other, the one who came to you before in the camp tent, she is my sister, Felisa."

59

"And Estralita Peralta?"

"She lives. She is the last of the Peraltas. My father wishes her dead." The girl frowned.

"You don't sound like you approve?"

"It is of no importance what a Marin woman thinks."

"It's important to me," Morgan said. He scooted up in the bathtub and did a half turn. His eyes met the girls and both knew what the other was thinking and what they wanted. Morgan had a flash of thought about her age but it passed quickly. He didn't give a damn about that either, as long as she was old enough to know her own mind.

Teresa Marin left the room. Morgan got out of the tub, dried himself and wrapped a towel around his waist. It proved to be a more modest act than any by Teresa. She was nude and on the bed and waiting. Morgan glanced at the door and back at her.

"It's allright," she said. "Everyone has been given orders to leave you alone. My father wants you to realize that he is a civilized man who has been wronged."

"Yeah," Morgan said, "I'm sure he does." He dropped the towel and moved to the bed. Hands reached up to welcome him.

Morgan's mouth began with Teresa's lips. He moved, slowly and sensuously down. Down along her throat, he kissed the indentations on each of her shoulders and let his tongue explore the cleavage between the modest but firm breasts.

Teresa wiggled and shivered with each of Morgan's movements and soon he had his hands working in conjunction with his mouth. He caressed her thighs, buttocks and paused at her hip bones when he got an extra reaction. He immediately moved down and let his tongue take over where his fingers had been.

Teresa Marin had been with a man before. Morgan felt less guilty but chuckled internally at himself. Certainly, he reasoned, there had never been that much guilt. He moved his hands up to her breasts and began to massage her nipples. They hardened at once under his touch and Teresa moaned with the joy of it.

Morgan moved down still further and let his tongue track along her inner thighs and finally come to rest on the black bush of her womanhood. This was no little girl. This was a woman and the scent alone brought Morgan very near to a climax. He had been celibate far too long.

He was so engrossed in giving pleasure and in turn feeling it by the very act he performed, he heard nothing.

The first realization of anyone else in the room came with a touch. A soft touch on his back, just between his shoulder blades. He thought nothing of it at first but then he realized it could not possibly be Teresa's hands. He stopped. He raised up and looked at Teresa. She was smiling and then her eyes shifted just a little to the left. Morgan turned his head. Felisa Marin was smiling at him, her hands still on his back. Her body naked.

"Holy shit," he mumbled. The two women now gently prodded and pushed Morgan until he was in the position they wanted him. He was on his back and the girls knelt on either side of him. Teresa began kissing his chest, his nipples, his upper abdomen. Felisa worked her wonders below that. She stopped short of taking him in her mouth but instead used her tongue with an expertise which Morgan didn't know existed outside of a whore house.

The number had been doubled, the sensation became astronomical. Two sets of hands, two sets of lips, two tongues, but with only one purpose, to give Lee Morgan total pleasure. The sisters seemed not only to sense Morgan's capacity but the limits of their own pursuits. Each time Morgan thought he was going to explode with pleasure, the sisters called a halt and changed positions.

They re-positioned Morgan lower on the bed. His legs were hanging over the end of it, his feet just touching the floor. Teresa Marin got on her knees between Morgan's legs, leaned forward and began licking him. Felisa had already climbed on the bed and positioned herself above him. He serviced her both orally and with his hands on her breasts. Unlike Teresa's tiny breasts, Felisa's were large, pendulous and highly sensitive.

Both women were moaning and Felisa's lips were grinding with the pleasure of every movement of Morgan's tongue. Still, they showed a self restraint which almost equalled Morgan's.

At the very height of their pleasure, they stopped and switched positions. Morgan was fast reaching a point of no return. Indeed, such a point was finally attained and Morgan couldn't help but wonder how they would split him up now.

Teresa straddled Morgan's face and Felisa assumed a similar position over his crotch. Between them, they kept his tongue, shaft and hands totally obligated to them. Teresa broke first, emitting a little howl of pleasure and writhing like a trapped animal. Her eyes were closed and her hands were busy on her own breasts as the pent up passion released itself.

Only a moment later, Felisa found release and Morgan couldn't hold out any longer either. Their bodies became one.

"Morgan," Teresa said, kissing his cheek, "next time you will make love to me." Morgan blinked. He was totally exhausted and the girl was talking about a next time. No, Morgan thought, not a girl, but two girls. He nodded, weakly. Felisa Marin slithered onto the bed beside him and kissed and nibbled at his ear.

"And next time," she said, softly, "I will feel your mouth on me."

They dressed and departed and Morgan downed two glasses of wine and smoked and thought about what had just happened and said aloud, "To hell with tomorrow." Lee Morgan climbed onto the bed and dropped into the deepest sleep he'd had in weeks.

# 5

Joaquin Marin ordered Morgan rousted out of bed well before sun up. As Morgan dressed, he pondered the realities which could face him when he faced Marin. He was none too sure about the discretion of either of Marin's daughters and he'd already considered his odds of escape. They were slim to none.

"I trust you slept soundly and comfortably, Mr. Morgan?"

"Very well," Morgan replied.

"Coffee?" Morgan nodded. "How do you take it?"

"Black, thanks." Marin handed Morgan the cup and at that moment Morgan decided to go over to the offensive. "The pistol is well hidden. It is in my possession. That is to say I have rather immediate access to it. I'll deal with you."

"You've made a very wise decision," Marin said. "I hope for your sake that you carry your end of it clear through."

"Believe me," Morgan said, "I fully intend to do just that." Morgan got up and served himself a second cup of coffee. He also helped himself to a cigar. Marin considered him. Morgan let the Mexican ponder him while he lit the cigar. Then he said, "A hundred thousand dollars, Marin. Fifty thousand to be hand delivered to me, right here, today."

Joaquin Marin frowned at first and then he smiled. "More of your Yankee humor?"

Morgan walked over, glanced out of the window and saw the man called Paco and his nameless shadow. Morgan refilled his coffee cup and turned around.

"Humor? Not hardly." Morgan gestured toward the window with a nod of his head. "Go ahead and call your monkeys, Marin. You've got plenty of them out there. Hell, kill me. You'll never see that damned pistol." He eyed the man and judged that he was making some headway. All he had to do now was to keep himself from rushing it.

"You think I won't order your death, Morgan?" Marin got to his feet. "I tried to be reasonable to you yesterday. I am not a man who gives his word lightly. I meant what I said. Give me the pistol and you will save your life."

Morgan strolled around the room with an air of total nonchalance. He looked at Marin's paintings, read a few of the book titles on the shelves and showed particular interest in an antiquated Spanish blunderbuss. Suddenly, Morgan turned around.

"I heard you yesterday, Marin, and I have no doubt that you'd order me killed in a heartbeat," he paused, "if you were a stupid man." Morgan smiled. "But you're not."

Marin moved toward the door. Morgan had anticipated him. He set his coffee down, walked to the window, pushed it open and hollered. "Hey, Paco. Your boss wants you in here. Right now!" Morgan, uncertain as to the amount of English the men understood, added a touch of sign language. Both looked stunned when Morgan pulled the window shut. Even before Marin could react to Morgan's action, the two men were at the door. They didn't bother with knocking.

Both eyed Marin and then Morgan. Morgan smiled, sipped his coffee and took a long, deep drag on the cigar. The scenario made no sense to the two strong arms.

"You had something to say to these uh, gentlemen, Mr. Marin?"

Marin, for the first time, was flustered. It turned to anger. He vented it on the men. "Get out! Get out and don't come unless I call you personally." They looked, for the first time, as stupid as Morgan imagined them. Both backed through the door. The advantage had moved to Morgan's side of the table. Marin glowered at Morgan and said, "Make no mistake, Yankee, you've won nothing. Nothing! Do you understand me?"

Morgan smiled and replied, calmly, "I'm not out to win anything, Marin, just negotiate the best damned deal I can get. He picked up the coffee pot. "Coffee?"

Marin walked back to the table. He took the coffee Morgan offered and then a seat. He looked up. "Perhaps I have underestimated you. Perhaps, we can discuss uh," he waggled a hand in the air, "some sort of arrangement."

Morgan pulled out a chair and turned it around. He sat on it opposite Marin, finished his coffee, ground out the cigar and said, "The discussion is over. Fifty thousand now, today," he jabbed at the floor, "here. The balance when you get the pistol."

"Don't push me too far, Morgan."

"And don't try treating me like one of your trained gorillas," Morgan shot back. "I'm no goddam U.S. Marshal. I'm a hired gun and a helluva lot better one than anybody you've got but the pickin's are getting slimmer every year. I'm planning to retire and that Peralta pistol with the fancy gold butt is going to make it possible. Now you take it or leave it."

"You don't know what you've got and neither do I until I see it."

"That may damned well be, but I know that what you've got now isn't worth a damn to you." Morgan was gambling now, pure and simple. He had nothing to lose. "You need the fourth grip, or you don't have shit!"

# PISTOL GRIP

"Your pistol has both grips?" The tone of Marin's question was one of excitement. It was also exactly what Lee Morgan had planned. If Marin had any of the grips at all, or the other pistol, this was Morgan's chance to find out. Marin had barely blurted out the question when he realized he'd been tricked. He leaned back, his face paled.

"The matching pistol? Is that what you've got, Marin? The Mexican no longer looked the powerful leader of a gang and the wealthy owner of a vast corner of California border land. Instead, he'd been slickered by an unknown gunsharp who'd ridden in from nowhere and was in possession of a sizeable share of one of the largest Spanish treasures ever recorded.

"I have only one grip." He looked up. "I was told that one pistol is missing a grip and the other has both." Bull's eye, Morgan thought. Marin had the grip he needed. The finishing hole looked promising and Morgan sure as hell had the right bait. Why stop now?

"The other pistol, Marin? Where is it?"

Marin looked up. He considered Morgan again but he decided not to tangle with him. At least not now and not with Morgan holding the high hand. "I'm not certain but I'm told it is in the hands of Estralita Peralta."

"And how do you know this Peralta woman is even alive?" Joaquin Marin looked up. His expression had changed somewhat. He didn't answer Morgan. Instead, he got up and walked to the door again. He put his hand on the doorknob but he turned back before he opened it.

"You may or may not be a lawman but you are certainly more than a trail dirty gun hand. You were both clever and resourceful this morning but don't press me. My family has waited for centuries to claim its heritage. Your arrival is a bonus I wasn't expecting so if I lose it, I'll be no worse off."

Morgan didn't need pictures drawn. He'd been too long at the poker tables to overplay his hand. He'd bluffed and it had raised the pot but now he'd been called.

"I don't give a damn about heritage," he said, "yours or the Peraltas or old family feuds. I told you what I want. Give it to me and I'll keep my end of the bargain."

"We'll see, Morgan," Marin said. "We'll see." After Marin left the room, Morgan cursed himself. Perhaps he'd already gone too far. He poured himself another cup of coffee and looked around until he found a bottle of brandy. He laced the coffee with a healthy dose and sat down to await the outcome of his charade. Morgan wondered how Marin knew about him and he was even more curious as to why the Winfrey name hadn't come up.

When Joaquin Marin returned nearly half an hour later, Teresa was with him. Morgan had to struggle to keep his eyes off of her. The once or twice he did glance at her, he was amazed at her restraint. Teresa bade Morgan a good morning when she came into the room but nothing else was said. Marin carried a leather pouch with him. He walked to the far corner of the room, removed several books from a shelf and exposed a wall safe. Morgan grinned to himself.

After the Mexican had locked the safe and replaced the books, he walked to Morgan and handed him the pouch. "Fifty thousand dollars, Morgan. Fifty, one thousand dollar bills, Yankee dollars." He smiled. "A great deal of cash, even for me." He jabbed at the pouch. "It's all there but you'll have plenty of time to count it. Now, Morgan, where is the pistol?"

Morgan tossed the pouch back to Marin and the Mexican caught it. The reflex action was good. Morgan noted it, assuming the man had equal skill with his guns. "I tell you where the pistol is, your men bring it back here and then you've got the pistol, the money and me. Shit! What the hell do you take me for, Marin?"

"The question, Morgan, is the exact opposite of that. What do you take me for? An easy mark? A good metalsmith could have made you a simple forgery."

"No offense intended," Morgan said, getting to his feet, "but it appears to me that we have a Mexican standoff." Teresa had been busying herself cleaning up the coffee cups and the pot. She stopped her work and eyed both men.

"Why not a compromise, Daddy?"

He scowled at her. *Señoritas* did not stick their noses into the business of their men. Morgan was at the window again. He turned around.

"Yeah, Marin, why not? You pick some men and you come along. Bring the rest of the money and I'll take you to the gun." Morgan pointed at Teresa. "She's your daughter, you must trust her. Let her take it to town and have it verified. You and I wait it out together."

"And what stops me from having you killed when Teresa returns?" Marin smiled.

Morgan smiled. "I will," he said, "because I don't ride one goddam foot 'til I get back my belongings. Horse, possibles and loaded weapons." Morgan walked straight to Marin. "You've got enough men to do me in," he continued, "and I'd likely only get off one shot. Guess who my target would be?"

"And what stops me from having you trailed and killed after we conclude our business?"

"I'll take my chances," Morgan said.

"Teresa!" The girl looked at her father and he nodded toward the door. She quickly gathered up the dishes and took her leave. "Morgan, I heard about you from a longtime friend. A man who himself was once connected to the Yankee gunfighter Wyatt Earp. Do you ride for Earp, or someone else?"

The question caught Morgan a little off guard. He thought he'd pretty well satisfied Marin's curiousity about him. Obviously that was not the case.

"I ride for Lee Morgan."

"It is a clever response from a clever man, but not a truthful one. I know there is more to you than meets the eye. Perhaps there is not the time to find out but I want to warn you. If you remain in this country, if I see you after our arrangement is complete, I will order you killed, or I will kill you myself. Is that clear?''

"Can't be much plainer," Morgan said.

"And one more thing, Marshal. I am not the only threat you face. My daughter did not lie to you when she spoke of the local sheriff in Holtsville or of Judge Lundsford and Don Miguel Carbona."

"That right?" Morgan feigned a lack of interest he sure as hell didn't feel but he knew if he was going to accomplish anything, he had to stay alive. That meant shaking off Marin.

# 6

Morgan knew full well the gamble he was taking when he made his deal with Marin. Morgan didn't have the pistol and, in fact, had no idea of when the Winfreys were liable to show up. He'd bought himself some time, nothing else. Now, as he rode in company with half a dozen of Marin's men, Teresa and Marin himself, Morgan was trying to figure out just how to best use that time.

He was not all that familiar with the country and was therefore limited on choosing a phony hiding place. He could sense Marin's impatience by the time they reached the road junction where he'd been captured.

"Hold up here," Morgan said. "You, your daughter and I will go on from here. She takes the gun and goes to town. You and I wait," Morgan said, "alone."

"I won't have Teresa going to Holtville alone."

"Why?" Morgan asked, sarcastically. "You didn't mind when you sent her in to con me?"

Marin scowled but held his temper. "There was no one else involved then. There is now. I won't have it."

"Then send a man or two with her. I don't give a damn. But when she comes back to us, she comes alone." Morgan could tell Marin didn't like it but he wanted the pistol even more.

"Very well. Teresa, after Morgan gives you the pistol, you will ride back here. Take Paco and Juan with you."

"Yes, Father."

Marin turned back to Morgan. "How far and in which direction?" Morgan smiled. "You never give up, do you? You just stay behind me. We'll head in the proper direction when we're out of sight of your men." Morgan didn't wait for approval this time, he spurred his horse and trotted off to the northwest.

His selection was not a random one. He recalled a dry stream bed he'd crossed when he'd first ridden in from Arizona. That arroyo seemed the most promising opportunity for him to make his break whenever he got the chance. Once he felt they were a safe enough distance from Marin's men, Morgan turned to the northeast.

They'd been riding for about a quarter of an hour and Morgan had still not seen a sign of the stream bed. Where in the hell was it? Maybe he had the wrong area completely. The country sure as hell all looked alike. He knew Marin would soon lose his patience. It came sooner than later. Morgan heard the lever of a rifle click behind him. He reined up, and did a half twist in his saddle.

"You've been giving the orders," Marin said, "for more than long enough, Morgan. I want the pistol. I want it now."

"It's under a rock in a dry stream bed just east and a little north. Not much farther." Joaquin Marin raised the barrel of the rifle until it was pointed at Morgan's head.

"You're a liar, Morgan. I think you've been lying to me all along but I know you're lying now." Marin put the rifle to his shoulder.

"Daddy."

"Shut up, Teresa! This man is lying." Morgan knew Marin had caught him, but how? Where had he gone wrong? Suddenly, it hit the gunman. He clenched his teeth, "Shit," he whispered to himself. He'd pulled a greenhorn stunt. "He is not stupid," Marin went on to Teresa, "and he would not hide so valuable a possession in a dry stream bed. A simple thunderstorm in this country could turn that bed into a raging torrent in minutes. Mr. Morgan is very much aware of that."

Morgan was like a little kid who just got caught with his hand in the cookie jar. Anything he said would only make matters worse. He had to gamble again. He shrugged. "I don't have the pistol, Marin, I've never had it. I hoped to get you isolated enough that you'd listen to a deal. I know where it is but I need help getting it. I figured I had a better chance out here than at your ranch."

Marin raised the barrel of the rifle just a hair and fired.

Morgan's hat flew from his head but the gunman was unperturbed. Now, his years of experience took over. He'd made a tactical error in his dealings with Marin, Marin had made a strategic error. Morgan's speed rendered the rifle, for all practical purposes, empty.

Morgan catapaulted himself out of the saddle, drew the Bisley and fired low all in the same motion. Marin took the hit high up on his left leg. The velocity was considerable at that range and the pain was intensified when the bullet cracked the bone.

Marin lost the rifle, grabbed for his leg and his horse reared in reaction to the proximity of the shot. Marin went down. Teresa Marin was wearing a gun. Morgan discovered she could use it but her own horse was even more spooked than her father's bronc. After rearing, it bolted and Teresa had to drop the pistol to stay on the horse.

Morgan literally leaped onto his own mount's back and took off in pursuit of Teresa. He knew there would be Paco and Juan and the others on his ass in minutes. He caught up with Teresa and she was spouting language the likes of which he hadn't heard since the last time he was short of funds in a house of ill repute.

He leaped from his own horse and took Teresa down.

*"Yanqui bastardo,"* Teresa screamed. She swung but Morgan was too fast for her and he didn't have time for the social graces. He cold cocked her with a right to the jaw.

Morgan reckoned that Marin's men would have easily heard the shots and riding hard would cover the distance in a third less time than it had taken him. His own mount had kept Teresa's horse from straying too far and he was counting on Marin's wound to pull off one or two of the men. He'd just have to deal with other events as they developed.

He held Teresa Marin in front of him and led her horse until they'd covered another couple of miles. He worked north but he wasn't certain that town was the place to go. At least not right away. Teresa was beginning to stir when Morgan stopped again and he decided to tie her onto her horse. By the time he'd finished, she was fully conscious. He took another moment to give her a drink of water and a warning.

"I've got no time for trouble, Teresa, so don't give me any or I'll put you back to sleep." She considered him but there wasn't much to think about. He'd done it once and she harbored no doubts that he'd do it again. She nodded passively.

Two shots rang out and Morgan saw the sand near his horse's hooves fly up. He looked back and saw two riders.

Morgan slapped Teresa's mount on the rump and the mare bolted off over a nearby hill. He freed his Winchester from the boot, chased off his own mount and turned to face the two riders. They were coming hard now, heads down. He smiled to himself. They figured him to run.

The first shot he fired was low, deliberately. The rider on the left reacted first, putting his horse into a half gallop and returning fire with his hand gun. The range was too great. Morgan's second shot took the man out of the saddle. Morgan didn't worry whether he'd killed him or not.

The second rider was good, very good. At full gallop, he unsheathed his rifle, worked the lever and with both hands free of the reins, raised the weapon to his shoulder. Morgan had no options to weigh. He killed the man with his third shot.

He didn't have to go far to find his own horse or Teresa Marin. He mounted up. "There will be more trouble in town and Paco and Juan will be coming after us. "I know a place, I've known of it for sometime." She swallowed. "You would have to go there sometime anyway. I will take you. Trust me, Morgan, I don't want my father in this. It is evil. The Peralta curse is upon that gold and my father refuses to admit all the truth of the story. Trust me."

"Where is this place?" Morgan asked, adding "and what is it, exactly?"

"It is just over the border in Mexico. A house. We can hide there and you can figure out what to do next." She looked back, nervously. Morgan knew she was right about one thing. Her father would send men swarming all over the hills looking for him and her.

"Whose place is it, Teresa? I don't need to trade one set of troubles for another?" Morgan frowned. "You said I'd have to go there eventually anyhow. Why?"

"To see Estralita Peralta."

The horizon blurred and the terrain between the riders and the horizon appeared to be undulating. The heat waves were distorting everything and the heat itself was taking its toll on both riders and mounts. Morgan had rationed the water by swallows when he'd learned that Teresa's canteen had been lost. It was nearing three o'clock in the afternoon, the very hottest part of the day, when the last of the water was used up.

"How the hell much farther is this place."

Teresa shook her head. Morgan thought she looked about ready to cry. "It's been so long. I," she paused and looked both right and left then dead ahead. "I'm just not sure. I'm sorry."

"Look, we must be close, if you're telling me the truth."

"I am, I swear it. I've been trying to get. . . ."

Morgan didn't let her finish. "Never mind that right now. You stay put. There's no use in killing both horses if we're lost. I'll ride ahead. You get under your mount, stay as much in the

81

shade as possible and I'll be back inside half an hour."

Morgan veered gradually east as he rode. He was acting on the best possible description of the terrain that Teresa could furnish. He was nearly ready to turn back when the wind carried to him the sounds of a barking dog. It was faint but it was real.

Two sizeable sand dunes separated Morgan from the sound but atop the second one, he saw the house. It was not unlike the Marin house in terms of the terrain. Several trees surrounded it and Morgan could see a well behind it. There was a creek flowing nearby, fed from the more frequent moisture which fell on the nearby Cargo Muchacho range.

Morgan eyed the spread carefully. There were two out buildings and the house. One of them served as a small barn and he could see there was some stock. The other was the biffy. There were no visible signs of human life but anyone with brains would be inside anyway. Morgan turned back to get Teresa.

All the way back, Morgan wondered to himself if he'd made another mistake. He'd gotten by with one earlier but he was not in a position to make another. If Teresa Marin was gone, he'd simply ride, hell bent, back to the little house and check it out. He was certain of Teresa's sincerity in only one thing. She'd gotten them lost.

Teresa was asleep and Morgan was relieved. He gently awakened her. "Any trouble?" She shook her head, rubbed her eyes and then used her blouse to mop the perspiration from her face and forehead. "I found it. Log, small, a small barn and a johnny?" She nodded and smiled. "Let's go," he said.

There was no one at the house but there was food, firewood and several items which attested to the presence of a woman. Morgan went straight to the well. He grinned when, after the third pump, water spewed from the spout. He filled two buckets and returned to the house. Minutes later, he was back at the well toting more. He made six trips altogether, thinking to himself that his present circumstance was as good a reason as any for not having gotten married.

Teresa Marin wanted a bath. She got one and then she wanted Morgan. She would have probably gotten him, too, but the owner returned. Estralita Peralta, Morgan decided, was all woman.

Estralita hugged Teresa as though they were long lost kin. Both had tears in their eyes. Estralita displayed little interest in Morgan at the outset. Finally, Teresa introduced them.

"So you are the famous Lee Morgan?" Morgan found it difficult to keep his eyes from roaming over her body. She had massive breasts, although not out of proportion to the rest of her. She was, Morgan reckoned, about five feet, eleven inches tall. Her legs were long, accounting for much of her height. The waist was narrow and the hips flared but again not out of proportion.

Estralita's face was almost angelic and the features were soft, presenting a molded appearance. Her lips were her most sensuous facial feature and she pursed them just right when she spoke. Morgan imagined them in other uses and felt the fire in his groin again. Here was a woman he wanted to bed, soon too, he thought.

They had looked each other over with almost microscopic detail. A fact that did not go unnoticed by Teresa Marin but Morgan thought she didn't seem to mind. His own thoughts went back to the Marin house and his experience with Teresa and her sister. He wondered if such a scenario could be repeated out here in the middle of nowhere with Teresa and Estralita.

"I don't know how famous I am," Morgan finally said, "but I am Lee Morgan. I sure as hell didn't know you existed, however."

Estralita smiled. "I asked them not to say anything. You might call me the final proof for the claims of Tad and Tammy Winfrey and Marshal Earp." She looked quizzical. "I heard you were a hired gun. I wanted the law on my side. I deserve it." Morgan showed her the badge.

"You know, I don't think it's too damned smart of you to live out here alone."

"I'm flattered by your concern," Estralita said, "but it's misplaced. I am not here alone." Morgan now sported the look of surprise. He'd made a rather thorough reconnaisance of the place and had not seen another living soul or any sign that anyone else had been near the place.

The door opened and a shadow filled the room, almost literally. The shadow moved and blurred and the room went into semi darkness. A great hulk, bending low to avoid a banged head, stepped inside.

"Morgan, meet Cho Ping." Morgan looked up and he kept looking up. There before him was the one biggest bastard Lee Morgan had ever seen. "Cho Ping was a Shaolin in China. He is seven feet tall and weighs nearly three hundred pounds."

"I retract my observation," Morgan said, "you're sure as hell not alone." Morgan smiled up at Cho Ping. He got no smile in return. Instead, the giant Chinese stretched out his right arm, touched Morgan's shoulder and then quickly slammed the arm, diagonally, across his own chest.

"He likes you," Estralita said, "and he approves of you being here and bringing the little Spanish flower. That's what he calls Teresa."

"I'm overjoyed that he approves," Morgan said. The girls both laughed. Morgan watched the big Chinese back out. He shook his head.

"Did you see Cho Ping's belly?" Teresa asked. Morgan shook his head. He'd been too busy looking up. "He was shot there once. Three times wasn't it, Lita."

"Yes, from some sixty feet away by a gunman. Cho Ping still ran the distance, zigzagging to avoid being shot again. He broke the man's neck in a single blow."

"Yeah," Morgan said, "the only stopping him would have to be a shot between the eyes."

"Easier said than done. He moves much quicker than you might imagine."

"I don't care to put it to the test either way," Morgan said. "Did I hear Teresa call you, uh, Lita?"

"Yes. All my friends call me that. It's my own choice and much easier than Estralita Madalena Desiree Lomacinda Lucia del Peralta."

Morgan shrugged, deadpanned her and said, "A little." It was the first laugh for any of them in sometime.

Feeling total security with Cho Ping standing by, Morgan rode off for nearly two hours just before dark. He was pleased to report on his return that he had seen no sign of anyone trailing them. After a hearty meal, Morgan made his contribution to the little party. He had a full bottle of bourbon and they all enjoyed an after dinner round of drinks.

"Tell me about the Peralta treasure," Morgan said. "Does it exist?"

"Yes. Up there," Lita said, pointing northeast, "in the Cargo Muchacho." She turned to Teresa. "Would you mind moving, please? Your chair, too." Teresa thought the request odd but she complied. "Do you have a knife, Morgan?" He nodded and handed her his Bowie. Lita poked a bit in the dirt floor until there was a sharp noise of metal striking metal. She probed and prodded some more and finally scraped away a three-inch layer of dirt. She handed Morgan his knife. "You will find a metal ring down there, Morgan. Pull on it."

Morgan put his back to it and finally a heavy door broke free and he slowly pulled it up. Lita stood nearby with a coal oil lamp. "There are snakes down there. Mostly harmless I think, but a rattler or two and plenty of scorpions." She handed him a long pole with a metal hook on its end. "Feel around with the hook until you detect a handle. Hook it and bring it up. It isn't nearly as heavy as the door."

The chest was wood and metal, somewhat resembling a stave barrel with one flat side. Morgan was reminded of the pirate's treasure chests he'd seen pictures of as a boy. This one was considerably smaller, however. Morgan cleaned it of dirt and cob webs and the placed it on the table.

"Its latch is no doubt rusted shut. Break it if you have to." He did and a minute later, he opened the lid. There was a small tray just beneath the lid. It contained a few odd looking chunks of gold and others which were obviously spear and arrow heads. They were also gold. Morgan removed the tray and found himself staring down at a piece of yellow oilcloth.

"You've seen the pistol the Winfrey's possess, of course." Morgan nodded. "It is rusty, aging and has one grip missing so I'm told."

"You are told right." Morgan eyed Teresa and then undid the leather thong tie around the oilcloth and opened it.

Morgan stared down, incredulous. Resting inside the oilcloth was a flintlock pistol with gold grips. Its condition was nearly perfect. "Damn!" He looked up. "Is that it? The real thing?" Lita nodded. Morgan reached for it and then stopped and looked up again. Again, Lita nodded. Morgan picked it up and scrutinized it carefully. He didn't really know what he was looking for, he was simply looking and thinking of the story the Winfreys had related to him.

"The barrel itself and the rest of the gun's frame are iron I guess but the plating, save for the grips, is silver, not nickel." Morgan looked at Lita. "As far as I know, the weapon is functional but, of course, its worth isn't in its value as a pistol."

Morgan put the pistol back into the oilcloth. "How long have you had it? How long has it been here? Where . . ." He caught himself and smiled. "You want to tell the story?" Lita smiled and nodded. Morgan glanced at Teresa.

"She has known for sometime about the pistol and its location. She could have told her father, she could have betrayed me. She has not."

"Why?" Morgan addressed his question to Teresa. "You did mention something about your father and all of the truth of the Peralta story. Is that the reason?" Teresa nodded.

"Enrique Peralta, the fourteen-year old

grandson of Francisco Peralta, walked out of the Cargo Muchacho mountains. I'm sure the Winfreys told you that much."

"Yeah, and they said no one knew for sure what happened to old Francisco or to the pistols."

Lita continued, "That is partially true. But we do know that Francisco kept one of the weapons. He gave his grandson the other."

"The kid buried this one," Morgan asked, pointing to the pistol.

"Yes. More than once. There was nothing here then, of course, but Enrique survived and determined that he would stay in this country, never returning to Spain."

"And that's how we end up with Peralta here." Morgan leaned back, poured himself some more whiskey and held up the bottle. The women declined. "I'm still listening."

"There are as many stories of what happened to Enrique Peralta as there are people to tell them. I do not think any purpose is served by repeating all of them and trying to figure out which one is the real one. The facts are somewhat more clear cut and simple."

Morgan drained his glass. "Yeah. We have two pistols, three gold grips which are supposed to be a map and a lot of greedy folks."

"Again, simply put," Lita said, "yes."

Morgan leaned forward and eyed the pistol and then asked, "How did we end up with so damned many players in the game? I mean outside of the obvious greed involved, the men

I've heard about or seen all claim ownership of the Peralta gold."

"As the writer would put it, Morgan, the plot thickens. First, *señor* Carbona."

"Uh uh," Morgan interrupted, waggling a finger in the air, "first we have the Winfreys."

Lita sighed. "Yes, of course, you are quite right."

Morgan smiled and added, "No climbing old family trees here, just simply put."

"Enrique Peralta's granddaughter married a Lutheran missionary named Josiah Winfrey. Enrique survived the rest of his family. The stories say he lived to be a hundred and nine years old." Lita pointed in several directions. "He is supposed to be buried out here somewhere, a few hundred yards away at most. This place was once the mission of Josiah Winfrey."

"Did old Enrique reveal the truth before he died?"

"We must assume he revealed some of it, certainly. It seems old Josiah considered the story a miracle from God. He went looking for the treasure. He found a rusty pistol."

"Okay, we have a Winfrey with a rusty pistol."

"Almost. Josiah died in the Cargo Muchacho. Indians perhaps, we don't know for sure. What we have is a Peralta who, by marriage, is also a Winfrey. And we have a rusty gun." Morgan pondered the story and said, "Let me hazard a guess. Our missionary friend didn't practice celibacy."

Lita smiled and shook her head. "He did not."

"So we have little Winfreys with Peralta blood. Now what?"

"A recognition of reality on the part of Mrs. Winfrey. The Winfrey name meant nothing. Most missionaries were not accepted at all. Those who were allowed to live were certainly not considered good business risks."

"She dropped her married name and we're back to the Peralta name."

"Quite correct. That name carried both legend and reality with it. Enter a business partner with money, Louis Encino Carbona."

"It's getting crowded," Morgan said.

"Very," Lita agreed, "and that doesn't even take into consideration the outsiders who heard the legend and came seeking the Peralta gold."

"We have Peraltas, Winfreys and Carbonas."

"And finally," Teresa said, "we have Marin."

Morgan shook his head. "Yeah. Hard as hell to keep it simple, isn't it?"

"Centuries produce people, Morgan. It is the way of the world."

Morgan grinned and said, "I know that but why the hell do all of them have to be looking for the Peralta treasure?" The women laughed. Morgan turned to Teresa. "Your daddy lays claim to it because the Marin family supposedly paid the fare for the Peraltas in the first place, simply put. True?"

"As far as my father cares to venture into the truth, yes. What he does not say," she looked down, Morgan sensed she was feeling shame, "what he does not say," she repeated, "is the fact that the Marin family in Spain took the Peralta fortune by force. Franciso Peralta wrote one letter back to his family after he'd found the gold. One of my ancestors was present when it arrived. Up to that time, they had been friends."

"But then, the Marin family took the Peraltas by force and sat back to await Francisco's return, gold and all."

"Yes."

"They must have had one helluva wait." Morgan shook his head at the turns and twists in the story but he understood now how a mix of legend and fact could prove a deadly lure.

"It sounds as though Carbona has more of a claim on a share than your daddy does," Morgan said to Teresa.

"I agree it sounds that way, Morgan," Lita interjected, "but this Carbona's father was as cruel and greedy a man as was Teresa's Spanish ancestors. He took the land to which our present day Carbona holds title, by force. He killed, brutally and ruthlessly to get it."

"Peralta land?"

Lita nodded and said, "Some of it. Two of the factions in the tale did make their peace and family branches no longer quarrel. They are willing to share the spoils of their victory."

Morgan looked puzzled now. "What factions and what spoils?"

"The Peraltas and the Winfreys. Recently, for the first time, the United States Supreme Court took up the issue of Spanish land grants. The Spanish were meticulous in that effort. Hundreds of maps and deeds exist. Some of them deal with bits of land barely more than five acres in size. Others cover vast regions which, if valid, would make some people the owners of entire states."

"Yeah," Morgan said, pondering Lita's revelation, "I remember reading about some of those decisions." He looked at the two women.

"Carbona lost his claim. So did Teresa's father."

"So they're going to do what runs in their families. Ignore the law and take it by force."

"Yes, Morgan," Lita said. "Once, I didn't believe the legend of the gold either. I didn't even care. Then, my father died and I found papers. Deeds and grants and his formal request to the courts."

Morgan saw the expression on Lita's face undergo a change and he could see the pain. "Your father, how did he die?"

"A fire. They say a horse kicked over a lamp in the barn."

"You don't believe it?"

"I don't know," she paused, "now."

Morgan pondered what she'd just said. "You spoke of a barn and horse. Your place?" She nodded. "Where is it?"

"Gone. It all burned. It was a windy night, very windy. There was no saving anything. The hands ran away. Most were peons. Two of my father's top men also died in the blaze," she took a deep breath, "supposedly."

Teresa Marin spoke up now. "I cannot bring myself to believe that my father would do such a thing or order it done. But I cannot deny the possibility."

"Either he or Carbona." The girls nodded.

"When all of this happened, I decided to ask for help. I received an offer on my land from Carbona and I was aware that he had made a similar offer to the Winfreys. The common denominator between us was Wyatt Earp."

"You made the contact and he got to the Winfreys."

"Yes. My father and their mother were kin too, by marriage."

"Their pistol and their father, Holt Winfrey. What's the tie there?"

"Much as you heard it from them, Morgan. Now of course, Holt Winfrey's death is also suspect and there is one other uh, well, story or legend or whatever you want to call it."

"And what's that?"

"This pistol has both grips, the Winfrey pistol only one. One story has it that Holt Winfrey subsequently came into possession of the fourth one. The story says he built the town of Holtville for two reasons. One as a base camp from which he could search for the Peralta gold. The other to hide the fourth pistol grip until he could locate the second pistol."

"You put any stock in the story," Morgan

asked, "either of you?"

Teresa Marin answered. "We don't know. Apparently my father does and so does Miguel Carbona. Our belief doesn't seem to matter."

"It matters a helluva lot to me," Morgan said. "And a few other things make more sense."

Lita frowned. "Like what?" she asked.

"Like a sheriff and two deputies in somebody's hip pocket. Whose?"

Teresa answered. "Indirectly, as I told you that first day, Miguel Carbona. But they take daily orders from Judge Lunsford."

"Uh huh, and just what the hell is his interest in the whole thing?"

"Why, he's filing the appeal to the Supreme Court to get them to overturn their decision. He's preparing evidence based on a precedent set on Indian lands. It has something to do with the law of Manifest Destiny."

"But in the meanwhile, he doesn't mind overlooking a few indiscretions or illegal acts committed by his client." It was a statement and not a question and Morgan looked worried. He finally looked up at both of the girls. "He is the most dangerous of the men we face. A helluva lot worse than any gang or fast gun or would-be dictator. Few men in this country wield more power than a Federal Judge." Morgan thought back to Wyatt Earp's insistence that he wear a badge. Now he knew why. "I also figure there's another reason for Lunsford and the sheriff."

"What's that?" Lita asked.

"What better way to keep tabs on a missing treasure and keep others with the same interest out or jailed or dead, legally!" The women looked at one another. Neither had considered that possibility. Teresa was more inclined to suspect her father of misdeeds than to suspect a man who wore the robes of a Federal Judge.

"My God! How do we fight that kind of power? What chance do we have?

"You fight fire with fire," Morgan said "and power with power."

Teresa considered him. "You have a plan then?"

"One damned good short term plan, yeah," Morgan replied. Teresa leaned forward in anticipation. Morgan smiled. "Let's get some sleep."

In the darkness, Morgan let his mind relax and soak up more slowly the vast amount of information he'd taken in. His thoughts were interrupted several times however, with visions of Estralita Peralta. He found himself wishing that he and she were alone in the shack.

Morgan closed his eyes and tried to sleep. He thought about Wyatt Earp and Tad and Tammy Winfrey. He chuckled. How had he ended up in no man's land looking for a damned pistol grip?

# 7

Morgan didn't mind riding away from the little shack. He knew the two women would be as well protected by Cho Ping as by Morgan himself. The trio had breakfasted together, in spite of the fact that it was still well before sunup. They had agreed that Teresa Marin would stay with them. If nothing else, it would keep her father engaged, believing her kidnapped by Morgan. If Morgan had any remaining doubts about Teresa, she virtually eliminated them with her private pledge to Lita Peralta.

Morgan pondered many possibilities after he rode away. He did not have a long range plan, he knew he must be ever alert to actions by those in the opposing camps and finally, he felt he could do little in the way of direct action until the

Winfreys arrived.

He did have one course of action, however, and he was determined to follow his own advice. Fight power with power. He had two methods in mind at the outset. Holtville boasted a tri-weekly newspaper. He would start there. His second stop would bring him into a direct meeting with Judge Arlo Lunsford.

When Morgan rode into Holtville, it was still early and as best he could, he stayed to the back of the buildings. He didn't want to attract any more attention than was necessary.

Morgan reached the office of the *Holtville Courier* and found it manned by a single individual. The man behind the desk didn't even look up when Morgan walked in. Instead, he motioned with his hand toward a chair and said, "Have a seat and I'll be with you in a few minutes." Morgan didn't argue but neither did he take the seat. Instead, he positioned himself where he could see the street.

He was still looking out of the window when the man finally looked up. "Jehosophat! You're Marshal Morgan, aren't you?" The title sounded funny to Morgan but he turned and nodded. "D'ja know there's a warrant out for your arrest? Sheriff Prather claims you beat up his deputies and may have gunned down two men in cold blood."

Morgan grinned. "That bad, eh?"

The man nodded and then wiped the palms of his hands on his ink covered apron. He stuck one of them out. "I'm mighty glad to metcha,

Mr. Morgan, yessir, mighty glad."

"I appreciate that," Morgan replied, "particularly in view of my first introductions to your community and the most recent news about myself." Morgan fished into the breast pocket on his shirt and withdrew a folded paper. "I know you can make more of this than I've written but that will tell you enough that you may get yourself a story out of it. Give it a try."

The little editor took the sheet and read it. His eyes grew bigger with each line and Morgan could feel a rejection coming. The editor looked up. "I'm Cyrus Black, Mr. Morgan, and if what I read there is the truth, you can be sure I'll print it. Can you substantiate it?"

"When do you go to press, Mr. Black?"

"Two o'clock is muh deadline, sir."

"I'll be back and you'll have your substantiation." Cyrus Black watched Morgan ride out of sight and then picked up the sheet of paper and read it again. He smiled. It would either assure him a lasting place in western journalism and put the *Courier* out front as a hard-hitting news source or it would get him run out of town. Or worse, he thought.

Morgan made no bones about his presence in town now. He rode down the main street and straight to the building which was used as a town meeting hall and, when the occasion arose, a courthouse. He knew he was being watched and at least two men went scurrying off in the direction of Sheriff Prather's office.

Inside, he found two small offices. One was

used by the court clerk and the other by Judge Arlo Lunsford. The court clerk leaped to his feet and started for Lunsford's office. The barrel of Morgan's gun slowed and then stopped him.

"You find yourself a hole," Morgan said, "and crawl into it until I complete my business with the judge." Morgan punctuated his demand by cocking the Colts. The man nodded and disappeared back into his office. Morgan pulled the door closed.

Judge Lunsford had heard some of the commotion and looked up but he was back to reading a transcript when Morgan walked in.

"You're either a very courageous man," Lunsford said, "or a very stupid one."

Morgan approached the judge's small desk. "While you're trying to figure out which, Judge, I suggest you hear what I have to say."

"I'm under no obligation to give an audience to a suspected fugitive."

Morgan once again drew and cocked the Colts. He leveled it at Lunsford's head and leaned a little forward when he spoke. "Yes, you are, Judge, in this case."

Morgan learned something at once about Judge Arlo Lunsford. He was not a man easily intimidated. He leaned back in his chair. "I can have you arrested or, if necessary, killed, Mr. Morgan, and when either one is done, no one will question me about it. If you live, you'll end up in Yuma prison. Killing me won't stop the process, except that if you lived, you'd hang."

"Alright, Judge," Morgan said, holstering

his pistol, "let's play it your way." Along with the badge Wyatt Earp had given him, Morgan had also received a formal letter of his appointment as a U.S. Marshal. He produced it now and tossed it on Lunsford's desk. The judge considered Morgan, glanced at the letter and finally picked it up. He read. As he reached the bottom of the page, he glanced up. The signature was far more of a threat to Lunsford than was Morgan's Bisley. It was signed by Lunsford's boss, the President of the United States.

Lunsford tossed the letter aside, feigning a nonchalance which Morgan knew he didn't feel. "Just who the hell are you, Morgan, and what do you want in Holtville?"

The gunman had gained a little edge and now readied himself to expand on it. He moved several things on the desk top aside so that he might sit on the desk's edge. That done, he said, "You know who I am, Lunsford, and you know why I'm here and it isn't to have you insult my intelligence by playing dumb."

Lee Morgan had only a pittance of book learning but the times and the land in which he'd been raised and now lived and worked, demanded a much more practical knowledge. At that, Lee Morgan was possessed of a Master's Degree. One of the skills he had honed to a fine edge was his judgment of men's reactions. He looked Arlo Lunsford square in the eye and let him squirm.

Lunsford's body, tense with the potential of a bloody confrontation, now relaxed, almost into a slump. It was more of a telltale sign of Lunsford's feelings than were his harsh words.

"You think you can walk in here with a letter you claim is a Presidential authorization and threaten me?" Lunsford chuckled. "I've seen your kind for twenty-five years in my courtroom, Morgan. You're barely more than a common drover with a skill for killing and a mentality to match." Lunsford reached for a silver box on his desk. Morgan tensed. Lunsford had, for a moment, made a judgment of his own. He lifted the lid. "Cigar, Morgan?"

Dammit, Morgan thought to himself, I had him and I lost him again. Morgan accepted the cigar and both men sized each other up, both plotting their next thrust or parry while they lit the cigars. Morgan made a sudden decision. It was an all or nothing at all plan but, he thought, I've still got the Bisley.

"I'm here to gather every bit of information I can on a man named Carbona. While my jurisdiction is unlimited, Lunsford, by virtue of this letter," Morgan picked it up and returned it to his pocket as he continued, "I am doing my work for the State Department. Our relations with Mexico have somewhat deteriorated of late and State seems to feel Carbona is responsible.

Judge Arlo Lunsford's eyebrows raised and his mouth opened and closed. He shifted his position in his chair. Morgan made certain his own demeanor remained stern but unchanged. Lunsford was calling on every ounce of his judicial experience. He was trying to view Lee

Morgan the way he always had to view a man in his court. Was he telling the truth or not?

"I don't believe you," Lunsford finally said. "I think you've got the gold fever, same as every other man of your cut." Morgan had him. He knew he couldn't lose a second in his follow up punch.

"I don't give a damn if you believe me or not, Lunsford. As to the gold fever business, that's simple enough. The whole Peralta legend gets me to the people I need to talk to. Beyond that, it's just bullshit." Morgan heard the front door to the building open and so did Lunsford. That, Morgan knew, would be the sheriff or his deputies or both. He stepped to one side, out of sight. "I heard you were an independent and totally uncooperative man but I like to make my own judgments, so I ignored what I heard. Apparently, I was told right. Well now," Morgan said, his tone again threatening, "I'm going to tell you something. You cooperate with me on my investigation, Lunsford, or I'll see to it you end up facing your own peers, in Washington. You'd better believe that!"

Sheriff Ty Prather and the deputy named Shorty burst into the office. Morgan grinned. Both men had their guns out and the instant they saw Morgan, they threw down on him.

"Damned good protection you've got, Judge. If I'd have been here for any reason other than what I've told you, there'd be three dead men in this room right now." Morgan pointed his finger at the judge and added, "And you'd

103

have been the first." The statement was both accurate and Morgan's *coup de gras.* Judge Arlo Lunsford had been baited, hooked and landed.

"Prather, you stupid twit! Did I send for you?" The sheriff's neck turned suddenly rubbery as he looked first at Morgan and then at the judge. Finally, he ended up scowling at his deputy. "Put those damned guns away and get the hell out of this office. You could have gotten me killed coming in here like that. Now get out!"

"He's a wanted man," Shorty said. Prather gasped at the audacity and stupidity of his deputy. Prather looked at Lunsford. Lunsford glanced at Morgan. He was very much aware of how foolish he was being made to look by the likes of Ty Prather. Morgan was very much in control. Lunsford forced a half smile at his sheriff.

"There has been a, uh, a little misunderstanding, Sheriff. If you will please, let me handle it." Prather stared and nodded.

After the sheriff's departure, Arlo Lunsford got to his feet. "What do you want from me, Morgan?"

"A commitment, first and foremost. I've taken the liberty of placing a story with the local newspaper." Morgan handed the judge a copy of it. "I told the editor I would be back in his office by noon today with your approval to run it. I hope you don't make a liar out of me, Judge."

Lunsford read it and Morgan watched his face. Morgan knew that if Lunsford could get away with it, he'd kill Morgan right on the spot.

He couldn't. He also couldn't refuse to acknowledge the newspaper story. It merely cited a State Department investigation into Mexican-American relations and offered up the district Federal Judge's full cooperation in the matter. Lunsford swallowed and Morgan knew he'd achieved what he'd come to do. He had Lunsford by the balls. Now all he had to do was squeeze.

Lunsford nodded weakly and handed Morgan the story. Morgan shook his head and said, "Keep it, Judge, for your file on the investigation." Morgan strolled to the door and then turned back. "I'll be in touch," he said. He walked out. Arlo Lunsford caught up with him some fifteen feet later. Morgan turned.

"If you've lied to me, Marshal, you're a dead man!"

Morgan returned at once to the newspaper office and found editor Cy Black elated with the judge's approval and commitment. He looked at Morgan however and said, "You know, this story could blow things wide open in Southern California, and it could also be your death warrant."

Morgan smiled and nodded. "So I've been told, Mr. Black. About a half a dozen times just this morning."

Cy Black considered him and then waggled the story in his face. "It could get us both killed but they won't look for any trouble out of me about it. They can shoot me, blow up my office or my printing press about anytime. You? Another matter. Watch yourself, Morgan. The good judge has got more than just drovers working for him."

"Thanks, Black. I'll remember."

In fact, Morgan didn't have to wait long for reminder. He'd decided to stay in town for awhile. For one thing, he didn't want to risk being followed and for another, he wanted to size up the competition. He was certain of one thing. One way or another, Judge Arlo Lunsford would try to do him in.

Morgan repaired to one of the smaller saloons along the main street to let the dust settle and await developments. He found himself the object of considerable attention, some of it, he thought, sincere but guarded.

" 'Scuse me, Marshal, like to buy you a drink." Morgan looked up. The man, he reckoned, was about fifty. He had the look of a ranch owner. A man who'd known his share of trial, tribulation and hard work but had prevailed. "Name's Lupton, Charles Lupton."

"Sit down, Mr. Lupton," Morgan said. Lupton sat. "What can I do for you?"

"No sir, Marshal, it ain't what you can do for me. If anythin', it's t'other way 'round. Course that kinda depends on the stories I been hearin.' "

"Such as?"

"Such as you bein' here to put Carbona an' Marin out o' binness. That true?"

"I'm not here to put anybody out of business," Morgan said. Lupton wrinkled his brow. "You might say I'm here to keep them from putting people out of business." The wrinkled brow disappeared and was replaced with a broad smile.

"Yessir, by God, that's what needs to happen awright. Yessir. Now then, Marshal, how many deputies you got ridin' fer ya?"

"Not a one, Lupton. I'm here all by myself." The wrinkled brow reappeared. "You tellin' me factual?" Morgan nodded. "Then, Marshal, yo're a by God bonafidey fool!"

"How many deputies do you figure I'll need?" Morgan asked.

"Carbona's got hisself close to a hunnert men ridin' fer 'im. Marin prob'ly half that many ag'in. You can kinda figger it out your own self."

Morgan considered the man and the facts. He'd known, of course, that both Marin and Carbona had plenty of men behind them but given his real reason for being there, he hadn't bothered to find out numbers. Now, he thought to himself, might be a good time to take complete stock of the enemy camp.

"You must have had something in mind when you asked to sit down here, Lupton. Assuming I had some deputies, what was it?"

"I could git some men to stand with you, Marshal. They be men who know 'bout fightin' an' ain't scared of it. Most are fair to middlin' shots an' can sit a horse an' take orders."

"And you'd be willing to get these men together if the need arose?"

Lupton got to his feet and shook his head. "I would o' been if'n I knowed they was somebody to lead 'em. Somebody who knowed what he was doin'."

"What makes you think I don't know what I'm doing?"

" 'Cause you come out here by yourself, Marshal, that's why."

Morgan stood up. "Before you make too hasty a judgment, Lupton, let me ask you a question." Lupton nodded. "How well do Carbona and Marin get on?"

" 'Bout as good as an ol' Blue Tick an' a bobcat. Why?"

"Just kind of curious," Morgan replied, nonchalantly. "Since they seemed to have about the same number of men riding for them, maybe I wouldn't need any deputies. Just a few men like yours standing by. If Carbona and Marin got mad at each other, looks to me like it'd keep 'em both busy. Maybe all we'd have to do is move in when it's over and pick up the pieces."

Morgan hadn't exactly come up with the idea stone cold. Several times he'd pondered the thought of open warfare between Carbona and Marin but he dismissed it for lack of a way that he could take advantage of it.

"Well, I'll be consarned," Lupton said, removing his hat and scratching the back of his head. "You be a mite smarter'n I took ya fer, Marshal. Yessir, a mite smarter. Besides, if'n you'd have brought deputies, they'd a tipped your hand sure. Bein' as how you're by yourself, I reckon Marin or Carbona either one is too worried 'bout ya."

"I don't know that I'd go quite that far,"

Morgan said, "but I would appreciate it if you would just keep quiet and wait 'til you hear from me, if you'd like to change your mind and help."

"You bet I will, Marshal, yessir. Now then," Lupton said, "I'm a friend o' Cy Black. He tol' me 'bout ya. Come time to git ahold o' me, he'll know how an' where."

"Good, Lupton, I'll look forward to it." Morgan shook Lupton's hand and watched him walk out of the saloon. It was, Morgan thought, one of the more positive things that had happened to him since he arrived in Holtville.

Morgan finished his drink, paid for it and headed for the door. The shot he heard was fired from some distance, but it had the easily distinguished crack of a high powered rifle. Morgan thought of a Remington Creedmoor.

Morgan hurried outside and saw a little knot of people about half a block away. Several of them were kneeling down. Morgan felt a twinge in his gut. He looked in both directions and saw no riders. He hurried down the street, arriving almost at the same time as Ty Prather did. Cy Black from the newspaper also came up. They all three pushed their way through the crowd.

"God, dear God. Poor Mary," Cy Black said. He looked at Morgan. "His wife." Morgan was still looking down. Down, into the face of Charles Lupton.

# 8

Morgan was fully aware that he was being trailed. He'd known it since he rode out of Holtville that morning. He'd stayed in town one day more than he'd planned, mostly to get a look-see at those who attended the funeral of Charles Lupton. There were many and most of the men in attendance looked like whipped dogs. Morgan reckoned they were not only mourning the loss of a friend but witnessing the burial of the only man who had shown any backbone and leadership.

He knew that Teresa and Lita would be beside themselves with worry but there hadn't been a damned thing he could do about it. There was no way to get a message to them and he considered it more important to snoop around as much as possible in Holtville. By the time of

Lupton's funeral, the word had spread of Morgan's presence and the alleged reason for it. The questions he was asking around town were all related to the line of bull he'd fed Judge Lunsford. Therefore, he was no closer to finding the fourth gold pistol grip.

Morgan rode nearly five miles out of his way to lead his trackers away from the Peralta shack. He also figured to double back on them and try to determine who they were and who was paying them. He didn't want a fight if he could avoid it. He couldn't.

Morgan ran his mount into a dry wash and then moved about a quarter of a mile away to an outcropping of rocks. By the time he got a good look at his pursuers, he realized that one horse carried only stuffed feed sacks.

"You can come down out o' the rocks, mister, or Slow Dog will kill you up there. It's no never mind to me." The man who was speaking now dismounted, slapped his horse on the rump and ran both animals about two hundred yards away. Morgan had been suckered but he didn't feel too bad about it. He'd been suckered by the best in the business.

As the man was shouting at him, Morgan heard the first noise he'd heard in the rocks. He turned slowly and found he was looking into the barrel of a rifle. Its owner was a full blood Apache. Morgan held his rifle up with one arm, stood up and began walking down the hill.

As he approached the second man, Morgan noted that he was not Mexican but American. He was big and mean looking. He was outfitted in buckskins and carried a single revolver

stuffed in his waist band. The man spoke in
Apache. Morgan's Apache was a little on the
short side but he picked up enough to figure that
he wouldn't ride out of here alive if the man had
his way.

"You an' me are gonna palaver, mister. Now
me, I'm gonna do the askin' an' you're gonna do
the answerin'." Morgan shrugged.

"You be Lee Morgan, that right?" Morgan
nodded. "Then I hear tell you're faster'n a rattler
with that there hip pistol." The man spoke to the
Apache called Slow Dog again and Morgan
heard the lever action work. "Now, Morgan, you
take hold o' that rifle o' your'n by both ends and
you put it up behind your neck." The man
grinned. "That'll keep them hands where I can
see 'em an' where you can't move 'em none too
sudden."

Morgan complied and then said, "You mind
if I sit?" The man in the buckskins shook his
head and Morgan crossed his ankles and sat
down, Indian fashion, on the hot sand.

"The fella what pays muh wages thinks he'd
like to do some palaverin' with you hisself. I tol'
him you was a lyin', no-good but he's a little
softer'n me. Anyways, we kinda reached middle
ground. I said I'd run you down and git the lyin'
streak outa you so's when he met ya, he wouldn't
be wastin' his time."

"Damned big of you," Morgan said. The
man moved toward Morgan and stopped when
he was about ten feet away. "Now it's a mite hot
out here an' I'm thirsty an' a shade irritable. I'd
sooner not have to work up a sweat to convince
ya, so when I ask, save us both a heap o' trouble

an' tell me the truth the first time. Ever' time ya don't, Slow Dog there is gonna git a sign from me an' you won't like what it means."

"Ask away," Morgan said, "I feel real truthful today."

"Where's the Peralta girl?"

"In a shack about eight, mebbe ten miles south of here." The man in the buckskins frowned. "That's mighty easy," he said.

"Truth tellin' is real easy when you've got an Apache at your back with a rifle and a man with your reputation asking the questions."

Another frown. "You think you be knowin' me, Morgan?"

"I'd make a guess. I'd guess you're Jessie Willow." The man grinned. "And I'd guess you're working for Don Miguel."

"Well now, I'm right flattered, Mr. Morgan, yessir, right flattered. Man with your reputation hearin' 'bout a no account like me."

"Don't feel too flattered," Morgan said, "there's a likeness of you in damned near every town south of the Canadian border and west of the Missouri River."

Jessie Willow's reputation could best be summed up in three words, cold blooded killer. Morgan was certain that Willow was the man who'd killed Charles Lupton. He was also convinced that Willow was his fastest route to Miguel Carbona.

"What you doin' wearin' law tin, Morgan?"

"I've got a connection or two who want a piece of the Peralta treasure. It's a helluva lot easier to move around when you're wearing a badge."

"Who are the Winfreys?"

Morgan had to struggle to keep his own expression from changing. He covered his surprise at the question with a cough. He looked up and he could see that Willow was expecting to hear his first lie. Morgan now reckoned that Willow wasn't asking any questions to which he did not already have the answers, or at least a damn good start to getting them.

"They're some kind of shirttail kin to the Peralta girl."

"How come they hired the likes o' you?"

Morgan detected a small opening. A chink in Willow's armor of knowledge. Morgan was betting that Willow didn't know about Wyatt Earp's connection. "The people I work for knew about them. That's the reason they gave me the badge. They figured the Winfreys would buy that quicker than anything else." Morgan smiled and shook his head in a gesture designed to add credibility to his answer. "They were sure as hell right."

"Where's the pistol with the gold grip, Morgan? An' where's Teresa Marin?" Morgan coughed again.

"The Winfreys have the pistol. Always have. The Marin girl is with the Peralta girl."

"An' the big Chinese fella," Willow said, grinning, "you jist walk right on by him, did ya?"

"Right now, the Peralta girl trusts me."

Jessie Willow considered Lee Morgan at length. Willow had made a promise of his own to Miguel Carbona. He would bring back Lee Morgan alive. Willow didn't want to incur the wrath of his employer, but alive left a great deal to Willow's imagination. He'd entertained visions of Lee Morgan being brought back, draped over a saddle with just enough life left in him to shake his head either yes or no.

"I'll tell you somethin', gunfighter," Jessie finally said, "that girl gives you a heap more'n I do by trustin' ya, but I'm gonna give a chanc'st to prove me wrong. Git to yore feet." Morgan strained a little to keep the rifle in position and still get back to his feet but he did it.

"What have you got in mind, Willow?"

"We're ridin' to that there shack and we're pickin' up them wimmin folk. Now when we git close, you'n me, we're gonna sit tight while Slow Dog moves on down an' slits that big Chinaman's throat."

Morgan turned suddenly and started walking. "Let's do it," he said.

"Hold up, Morgan." Morgan stopped and turned around. "I won't kill ya. I mean if I find you been lyin' to me, I won't kill ya but I'll promise ya, you'll wish I had of." Morgan eyed the big man but said nothing.

"You un'erstan' me, gunfighter?" Morgan nodded. "Say it."

Morgan was getting fed up with Willow but he clenched his teeth.

"I understand you, Willow."

"Now one more thing. You toss that rifle to me, real easy an' careful like an' after you done that, you unbuckle that there gunbelt." Willow pointed and added, "With yore left hand."

Morgan was about midway between Willow and the Apache. He was in a half turn where he could see them both with his peripheral vision. He'd first considered the possibility of making his move after they got to the shack. It was too risky and he wondered why he'd even considered it. The Apache might just do to Cho Ping what no one else had been able to do, kill him. In any event, if there was one slip up on Morgan's part, it would be too late to correct it.

"Here you are, Willow." Morgan let the Winchester slip into his left hand and he gave it a sudden toss, but a weak one. Jessie Willow's reflexes, Morgan reckoned, would do the rest. Rather than letting the rifle go, Willow would make an effort to catch it. At the instant Morgan moved his left arm to toss the rifle, his right one, which was on the Apache's blind side, moved in a blur of speed. Morgan drew, did a half twist and a drop to the ground as he fired. The Apache still managed a shot but it was harmless. He took Morgan's bullet between the eyes.

Jessie Willow realized the error he'd made even as he was making it. He also realized that a man didn't make an error when he was facing Lee Morgan without paying the price. The price Jessie Willow paid was the highest any man can pay, ever. Morgan's shot pierced Jessie's heart. The huge man's eyes bulged out and he glanced down at his chest as though he could will himself another chance. He staggered, he blinked and his knees buckled beneath him. Still, he reached for and drew his pistol and as he fell forward, he fired into the ground.

It took all Morgan's strength and the help of a rope and his horse to load Jessie Willow onto the back of his own mount. Morgan didn't bother with the Apache. He covered him with a few rocks but took his headband. It would be proof enough when the time came. Morgan also felt a new and deep anger. He found a rifle boot on the Apache's horse. In it reposed a Remington Creedmoor. The Apache had done the dirty work but it was Miguel Carbona at whom Morgan's anger was directed.

He arrived at the shack, relieved to find it and its occupants intact. He quickly explained what had happened in Holtville, who was involved and then what had happened on the trail. The women both had the same question. What next?

"We're pulling out of here, right now. Jessie Willow knew more than I had a chance to find out but if he knew some, you can bet Carbona knows even more."

"But where can we go?"

"I had an invite to stop by the Lupton place tomorrow evening. There's going to be a meeting of some of the landowners. We're going to be there."

"Morgan," Teresa said, "how can you be sure about all of those people? What if my father or Carbona has spies among them?"

"Yeah, Teresa, I thought about it and you're right. We don't know who we can or can't trust. Thing is, we're never going to be sure until we get out of here. We can hide from now on or we can make a move. Which way do you want it?"

Teresa looked at Lita Peralta. Their eyes both told Morgan what they were thinking. The time for safe choices had come and gone. Besides that, he had to be back in Holtville quickly. The next stage was due to arrive in two days and it was more than likely that it would be carrying Tad and Tammy Winfrey.

Lita glanced out of the window and eyed the motionless form of Jessie Willow. She turned back. "What about him?"

Morgan smiled. "I'm sending him home. We'll be within five miles of Carbona's compound. The horse will do the rest."

Charlie Lupton's spread was one of the prettiest in the area. Morgan found it hard to believe the lush green surroundings were, in fact, in the middle of such desolate and otherwise barren terrain. The physical layout of the ranch put him in mind of his own home in Idaho, the Spade Bit. He grimaced each time he remembered that he no longer had a home. The Spade Bit had been burned out once and for all. Lee Morgan was a loner. No father, no mother, no living kin of which he was aware.

Lita Peralta's query jarred Morgan's daydream. "What if they don't want us and won't let us in down there?"

"Then we'll have a little better picture of where we stand in this thing." He looked at both women. "You go on ahead a ways. Any lookouts they've got posted will let you get closer than they would a man. Cho Ping and I won't be far behind."

The girls rode off, tentative about it, and both glancing back several times to reassure themselves that Morgan and Cho Ping were not too far behind. Morgan finally called a halt for him and the big Chinese. Cho Ping's head jerked around and he stared a hole through Morgan.

"I just wanted to tell you my idea. You stand guard at the corral. Anybody tries to ride out early, you stop 'em."

Cho Ping's expression rarely changed. Morgan had inquired of Lita about her reference to him as a Shaolin. Morgan learned that the Shaolin was a religious order which stressed physical as well as spiritual training. Somewhere in his training, something went wrong and Cho Ping had violated the Order's strict rules and was banned.

Now, the big Chinese grinned broadly. He held up his left arm and gripped it, high up, with his right hand. "No one will leave until you say." Morgan wasn't sure about Cho Ping's change toward him but he was damned grateful for it. They rode into the Lupton spread.

Morgan found the ranchers had posted two lookouts. Any greenhorn could have taken them out however. Too, with almost no questioning, they accepted the quartet inside. Morgan knew there would have to be many changes if this small band of human beings was going to stand up to the likes of Carbona and perhaps Marin as well.

Morgan sought out Mary Lupton and explained how he came to be at the meeting, how he had met her husband and that her husband's murderer was now himself, dead. It was, Morgan thought, damned little consolation but Mary Lupton struck him as a woman who had as much courage as that possessed by her late husband. Indeed, after she listened to Morgan's brief story, she proved it.

"We're holding the meeting in the barn, Marshal. I want you to come out there and let me introduce you and I want you to tell these people what you just told me." She smiled. "As to these girls, they're both welcome in my home and they can stay as long as it's necessary."

"Ma'am," Morgan said, "I appreciate it and so will they but I don't want you underestimating the dangers I mentioned. They are many and imminent."

"Dangers?" She smiled, wistfully. "I just lost my husband, Mr. Morgan, and without a fight, I'll lose my home. The danger I feel is in not doing anything about it."

While a few of the men in the gathering were hired hands, most were land owners and ranch operators. The Peralta gold, if it did exist, was of little importance to them. Their land and homes and families came first and they were ready to fight if they felt they had a chance. The problem seemed to be that most of them felt they did not.

The unofficial spokesman for the group was the owner of a small cattle operation. His name was Howard Leeds and he was in company with a couple of seedy looking gunslingers. Men he'd hired as personal bodyguards. One of them, Morgan noted, had been whispering to Leeds throughout much of the meeting.

"That there is real purty talk, Mr. Morgan," Leeds finally said, "but it don't say much. We're facin' two big powers here, Carbona and Marin, and by what I can figure, they got the only law that matters." Morgan was sizing the man up but Leeds wasn't through. "Besides that, I hear tell you ain't really no marshal." That one caught the attention of the gathering and a hush fell over them.

"Who told you that?"

Leeds ignored Morgan's question and continued. "What I hear is that you'd hire your gun to the man with the most money to offer. I hear your daddy was a killer name o' Frank Leslie." Leeds looked around, feeling the mood of support for his allegations. Leeds looked back at Morgan and added, "An' I hear tell the only reason you came here was to look for the Peralta gold. Now whatta you got to say 'bout those things?"

"Only one. There's a war brewing in this country and everybody in this room is going to be in it, unless they hightail it out of here tonight. Like any war, as soon as it starts, nobody gives a damn anymore about what started it. When this one starts, you'd better be gone or you'd better be ready to fight."

"You didn't answer his questions," someone shouted.

"The answers are none of his damned business."

"I'm makin' it my business," Leeds said, "I won't ride for no gunslingin' killer."

"Then I'd suggest you ride out, Leeds, right now." Mary Lupton pushed her way through the crowd and moved up beside Morgan. She scowled at Leeds.

"How dare you speak like that to this man?" She pointed to the two men who were in Leeds' company. "Your wife didn't even want you to hire those men you've got on your payroll and four of your best, hardest working hands rode away because of them.''

The two men now separated and so did the crowd. Mary Lupton sucked in her breath. Morgan had already sized them up. As a matter of fact, he knew one of them. A gunny named Jake Branch. Morgan had killed his cousin in a gunfight in Idaho some five years earlier.

"Move behind me, Mizz Lupton," Morgan said, calmly.

"But, Mister . . ."

"Now, Mizz Lupton!" She moved. "That's far enough, Branch."

Leeds eyed the two men and frowned. "No trouble, boys, I don't want no trouble. I just think we got some answers comin'." It was the man named Branch who responded. "Shut up, Leeds! Morgan there is the reason I hired on. The reason I come."

"What? Now just a minute here, Branch, I give the orders and you take 'em."

"Not no more, Leeds," Branch said, "an' I won't tell you again, shut up!" Branch grinned and addressed himself to Morgan. "Want you to meet Billy Baines. Best little gunhand you'll be likely to see fer the rest o' your life, Morgan, which ain't gonna be too much longer. Boys!" Branch was yelling to three more men who were supposed to have slipped in and positioned themselves in the loft. They had ridden there for the specific purpose of breaking up the meeting. It was as Morgan had figured, they were plants. It made no difference whether they worked for Marin or Carbona.

Branch got no answer to his cry. He tried

again. "Boys!" This time, he got an answer. Three bodies tumbled from the loft. They were clad only in their longjohns and they were hogtied and gagged.

"No boys," Cho Ping said.

Jake Branch's eyes got big and round and his jaw dropped open. He turned, looked up at Lee Morgan and said, "No, Billy boy!"

Billy Baines was barely twenty years old but the cut of his rig told Morgan he was the fastest of the two men by far and away. Morgan's eyes had never really been off of Billy.

Billy Baines blinked and drew and fired. He put a bullet through a lantern about two feet above Morgan's head. Morgan drew and fired and didn't blink. That was the only difference, almost. The other difference was Morgan's bullet. It went through Billy Baines' heart.

Morgan could have easily killed Jake Branch as well. He had plenty of time but Branch had an odd expression on his face, his right hand at the back of his neck and he was falling forward. Closer examination proved that his spinal column had been severed just at the base of his skull.

As Morgan and some of the other men were examining him, Cho Ping walked up. He knelt down and his powerful fingers withdrew a star shaped piece of metal from Jake's neck. Cho Ping held it up, smiled and said, "Shurikan."

# 9

The presence at the meeting of five men intent on killing Lee Morgan gave Mary Lupton the boost she needed to gain support for her "stand and fight" movement. Morgan found himself elected to the leadership by unanimous vote. It was a role he didn't want, but it offered a thin veil behind which he might carry out his real purpose.

The day had been long and harrowing and Morgan was glad when he was finally able to retire to the privacy of his own room. He'd agreed to stay on at the Lupton place until the stage's arrival.

He lay back on the bed and pondered the difficulties of his new role. He knew it would make his search for the treasure that much more difficult and any agreements with Marin or Cabona totally impossible. Under his breath, he was cursing Wyatt Earp as well as his own need of money.

The soft rapping at his door didn't bring the usual reaction. Somehow, he felt perfectly safe for the moment.

"Yeah?"

"May I come in, please?" The voice was barely audible but Morgan recognized it as Lita Peralta's. He sat up, rubbed his eyes and noted that he had a small headache. He squeezed the bridge of his nose between his thumb and forefinger.

"Yeah," he replied. He got off the bed and walked across the room to turn up the lamp. He didn't get to it.

"Please," Lita said, "leave it dim." Morgan turned to face her. She had on a very revealing, silk nightdress. "I wanted you to know how grateful I am, Morgan. I didn't want to wait because I don't know what the future will bring, but I am ever so grateful to you." A single tie string held the nightdress together. Lita untied it and the frock slipped from her creamy shoulders.

Lee Morgan lived his life by only a few hard rules. One of them dictated that there was a time and a place for everything and he knew that neither one was right for this. He also lived by the edict that states, for every rule there is an exception. He sucked in his breath at the beauty which stood before him and realized the latter rule prevailed in this case.

Estralita Peralta's body radiated heat and a musky, feminine odor which, of itself, could arouse a man. Morgan quickly forgot his aching muscles and mental concerns. Lita straddled him, leaned forward and began brushing his cheeks and lips with the mountains of flesh that were her breasts. Lita's nipples were soft and pliable but quickly hardened.

"Lick them," she said to him, softly. He did and she moved to alternate between them. She held remarkably still for him and manipulated the mounds to extract the maximum sensation from Morgan's efforts. Soon, Lita was breathing faster and heavier and she pulled away from him.

She repositioned herself and began kissing and licking Morgan's bare flesh, his chest and down along the center of his stomach. She worked lower until she could make contact with his manhood. She did and it was Morgan who was squirming. Lita pressed tighter against him, mostly in an effort to get him to lay quietly and enjoy what she was doing.

After a somewhat longer period of time than Morgan had spent on Lita's breasts, she got up again. She leaned forward and kissed him on the mouth and let her body slide down against him. They seemed to fit together perfectly and Morgan found a new sensation as the mass of Lita's public hair scratched and rubbed against his erection.

Lita finally rolled to her back and held her arms out until he filled them. They kissed and then Morgan resumed his oral ministrations on Lita's body. These exchanges of pleasure continued for nearly an hour. By then, both parties were at the very peak of their endurance. Lita Peralta pushed Morgan away, sat up, turned around and got on her hands and knees.

Morgan knew what to do and he did it and Lita moaned, writhed and seemed to find a whole new physical sensation to the act. It ended in a sweat soaked merger of two naked human forms whose sole purpose was to give and receive physical pleasure.

Morgan and Lita parted with a kiss usually reserved for the likes of a courtship but both had felt something very special between them. Neither spoke of it but both thought it went beyond the usual sexual experience. Morgan butted his cigarette and got into bed. He smiled as he wondered how much more grateful Lita might be later on, and if he'd be able to accept her expression of it. He dropped off into a deep sleep.

While Lee Morgan was accepting a somewhat unorthodox display of appreciation for a job he'd not yet done, Holtville Sheriff Ty Prather was arriving at his office. He was bleary eyed and not a little irate at having been summoned from his bed at such an unholy hour.

"Who the goddam hell is so important that they figger to pull me out o' bed at this time o' night?" The sheriff was speaking to the boy who'd brought the message to him. The lad now stood, hand out, waiting his pay. Prather looked at him and scowled. "Let him what sent ya pay ya boy. He owes ya."

The door to Prather's office opened and the sheriff looked up. A man said, "Pay the kid, Prather, and get in here." The sheriff swallowed, nodded and took out a quarter. "Give 'im a dollar, that's what he was promised." Prather swallowed and reached for a dollar. A moment later he stepped inside.

"Long time no see," Prather said, tentatively.

"Not long enough to suit me, Prather," the man replied, "but I didn't come to see you, just to give you a little advice."

Prather smiled weakly and said, "Little friendly advice never hurt no man."

"I didn't say it was friendly, Prather. Healthy advice is more accurate. The stage is due in later today, that right?" Prather nodded. " 'Bout eleven o'clock is usual."

"Leave town at ten-thirty, Prather, and take those mealy mouthed no-goods you call deputies with you. Stay gone until sundown."

Prather frowned. "Where am I s'posed to go?"

"I don't give a damn where you go, just make sure you're not inside the city limits of Holtville."

"I, uh, I'm not sure I can do that without . . ."

"You can do it or I'll kill you. It's up to you.

You can either make yourself scarce or make yourself dead."

The man giving the orders to the Holtville sheriff was a gunfighter named Brock Haskell. He was one of the most feared men in California and possessed of the skills to keep it that way. Haskell was known to have murdered at least fifteen men in his life and had stood trial in the deaths of at least six of them. He'd received a verdict of acquittal in all six cases on a plea of self defense.

Haskell wore a customized Smith & Wesson, .44/.40 in a vest holster. He drew left handed and was credited with having faced down famed U.S. Marshal Billy Tilghman in an El Paso brothel.

"Damn, Mr. Haskell, I git muh orders right here in town an' I'd be in a dung pile if I did what you say without checkin' first."

"You've been warned, Prather, and that's what I came here to do but I'll remind you of something."

"What's that?"

"A dung pile beats the hell out of a pine box."

Ty Prather left his office and headed straight for the Lazy L ranch, the Lunsford spread. The judge was none too happy about being yanked from his bed either but he listened to the nervous little sheriff's story.

"I figgered you oughta know. Whatta ya want me to do?" Judge Lunsford gave Prather a pitiful look. "Just exactly as you were told, get the hell out of town. Haskell is, uh, on the payroll temporarily. He's going to handle a little job for us. Didn't he tell you that?"

Prather shook his head. "Never said nuthin." Every now and again, Ty Prather found a threadbare swatch of courage deep within himself. Most of it came from being in the employ and therefore confidence of a Federal Judge. He experienced just such a bravado at this moment. "Ya know, I'm on the payroll too, so to speak." He smiled, weakly again. "If they is a job to do, I'd reckon I ought to git first crack at it."

Judge Lunsford was in no mood to be amused but he couldn't resist a little smile at Ty Prather's veiled demand.

"Fine," the Judge said, "ride back and tell Haskell to forget it, that you'll handle it personally."

Prather bit. He smiled. "Sure Judge, sure. Uh, jist what is the job?"

"Kill Lee Morgan."


Sunrise was accompanied by a desert shower. They were infrequent and even the rain drops were hot but they settled some of the dust and gave the air a clean, fresh scent.

"Mornin', Mr. Morgan." Mary Lupton was pouring a cup of coffee with one hand and gesturing toward the table with the other. Morgan was surprised she was up and his look showed it. She smiled. "I've been gettin' out o' bed about four of a mornin' for nearly thirty years now, an' fixin' breakfast for a passle o' ranch hands or muh own man or both. Don't go spoilin' it for me by tellin' me you don't eat in the mornin'."

"I won't, Mizz Lupton."

"Mary is muh name, I'm not comfortable with anythin' more'n that." Morgan nodded. He heard footsteps and reached for his gun. "It's that big Chinese fella, Cho Ping. He was up when I come down." She smiled as she served up Morgan's eggs and said. "Now there's a man any woman ought to really enjoy cookin' for. He ate a dozen eggs, fifteen flapjacks an' two pounds o' hogback easy."

Morgan looked up, grinned and said, "Then, you've cooked breakfast for one man this morning and one kid." He held up two fingers, "I'll have two eggs, three flapjacks and about two medium thick slices of hog back." She laughed. Morgan liked her. She put him in mind of Idaho and his mother when she used to flit around the kitchen. He ate and as he did so he was aware of Mary Lupton's enjoyment in watching him.

"Morgan," she said suddenly, "I'm not usual a woman who sticks her nose where it might not fit but there's somethin' I think you should know."

Morgan was finishing off the last of his flapjacks and he washed them down with a swallow of coffee and then said, "What's that, Mary?"

"I don't think you know how much of an impression you've made on the Peralta girl. Oh, I know she's got some troubles right now but there's a look on her face I've seen before." Mary smiled. "Had it on my own once." She frowned. "Just don't be too hasty to chase her away if she comes 'round wantin' to say thanks."

If Morgan had been given to blushing, it was a perfect opportunity. As it was, a hasty departure suited him better. He looked at Mary Lupton, smiled and said, "I promise, I won't be hasty."

Morgan gave a few last minute instructions to the Lupton ranch hands and said his farewell to Cho Ping. Mary Lupton came out on the porch as Morgan was mounting up.

"Don't you go an' get yourself shot up, Morgan. We need you. Just meet that stagecoach and get those young people back out here as fast as you can."

"I will, Mary, and tell the girls to stay put and stay close to Cho Ping." He pointed to Mary. "And you do the same."

The same sunrise brought Judge Lunsford, for the second time, to his front door. He was prepared to give Sheriff Prather a sound reprimand. Instead, he found himself staring into the ugly, bearded faces of three vaqueros. The ugliest of the unsightly trio proved to be the spokesman.

"*Buenos dias, señor* Lunsford." He stepped aside and pointed toward the yard. "We have your *caballo* ready and Don Miguel awaits you."

Lunsford frowned, "I'm not riding out to see Don Miguel at this hour or, for that matter, anytime today." The big Mexican turned back,

smiled and telegraphed a meaty fist into Lunsford's middle. The judge crumpled into a heap at
the Mexican's feet.

"Juan, some clothes for the *señor.*" Lunsford moaned. The Mexican named Juan went
inside and stood admiring the home's interior. A
moment later, Lunsford's wife appeared at the
head of the stairs.

"Who are you?" she shouted. "And what do
you want?" Juan didn't answer but started up
the stairs. Mrs. Lunsford started backing up.
Judge Lunsford got to his hands and knees and
looked inside.

"No," he said, weakly, "leave her alone, I'll
ride with you." Lunsford's wife backed into their
bedroom. Juan followed her. "Jeanette," Lunsford screamed, "give him my clothes."

The judge's wife darted across the room to
the closet and pulled down a pair of pants, a shirt
and some shoes. She threw them on the bed and
then hurried to the chiffonnier and found some
socks and a pair of galluses. When she turned
back, Juan was right in front of her. She stifled a
scream and held out the items. Juan pushed her
arm aside.

Downstairs, Judge Lunsford got back to his
feet with the help of the doorknob. He was
wobbly but he stepped inside and shouted again.
"Jeanette! Jeanette, are you all right?" He
turned and looked at the man who'd hit him.
Lunsford's look was missing the usual arro-
gance. His eyes were pleading.

Juan reached up, gripped the neckline of

Jeanette Lunsford's nightdress and pulled. It fell away like rotting lace and Juan stood licking his lips and taking in her total nudity with his eyes while she screamed. Downstairs, the judge turned and made two quick steps toward the stairs. The big Mexican unleashed another blow. This one to Lunsford's right kidney. The judge groaned, staggered and went down again.

"Juan, come, we must go." The scream stopped. Judge Lunsford felt hands pulling him to his feet. His clothes struck him in the face and fell to the floor. The Mexican picked them up and Lunsford saw Juan coming down the stairs, smiling. "The *señora's* teats, they are *magnifico señor.*"

Judge Arlo Lunsford had, at one point in his career, been one of the most promising members of the American Bar Association. He had been a strict disciplinarian and was possessed of one of the keenest legal minds in the country. There were even rumors of his consideration to the Supreme Court, easily its youngest member.

Things began to go sour for Judge Lunsford after a half a dozen unsuccessful business investments and a very costly mining venture. Soon, it was money and not justice which dominated Lunsford's decisions. The judge's connection with Miguel Carbona seemed to ease Lunsford's immediate needs. Thereafter, the temptation was for bigger and better, at any cost.

Now the Carbona relationship was coming home to roost. Carbona had placed great stock in

Judge Lunsford's promises to find the missing pistol grip. Carbona knew something else about its hiding place which no one else knew. There were, hidden with it, the names of those who had the two pistols.

Carbona had been patient and Lunsford had been stalling. He knew nothing more now than he had months before but there were new problems. New faces were appearing and now a fast gun with badge to back it up. Carbona wanted action and he had run out of patience. He sent his men to fetch Lunsford to him.

"You are looking peaked, *señor* Lunsford," Miguel said. He gestured to his men to leave them alone. "Have you not been feeling well?"

"You cannot send your dogs to my home and abuse my wife and assault me. You forget who I am, Miguel."

"Tsk, tsk," Miguel shook his head, "is that what happened this morning, *señor*? I shall speak to the men. Those who are guilty will be properly punished, I assure you." Lunsford knew it was a lie but discretion was definitely in order. "I know you must have missed your breakfast. Will you join me?"

"I'm not hungry," Lunsford said, "and I have a busy schedule. I would appreciate conducting our business and being on my way."

Carbona could not be hurried. He carefully tucked his napkin into his shirt collar, sampled his eggs and sent them back to the kitchen because the whites were not cooked to his liking. He sipped fresh orange juice and silently offered

Lunsford some coffee.

"You have been a disappointment to me, but I have displayed to you my generous understanding of your problem." Miguel looked up, smiled, reached inside his tunic, producing a throwing knife and placed it on the table.

Judge Lunsford was a man who understood threats and physical violence and was not easily intimidated by the mere threat of them. The earlier incident of course had been more than a mere threat. Lunsford did understand Carbona, however, and fully realized that Carbona would not hesitate to use physical violence, even to its ultimate end.

"I have failed to deliver as promised, Don Miguel, but I need only a little more time. I expect developments to take a sudden turn and when they do, we will have all of the information we need."

"You mean from the marshal with the fast gun? You can handle this one?"

"Of course I can," Lunsford lied, "I deal with his kind in my court room every day."

Carbona took a huge bite of egg and toast. Yoke dribbled down his beard. He took a swallow of coffee, swished it around to loosen the bits of food stuck to his teeth, swallowed it and then wiped his beard.

"Why then," Miguel asked, smiling, "did this man come to your office and threaten you and you let him get away with it?"

Lunsford assumed that Prather had ridden directly to Don Miguel and told him everything.

His assumption was partially correct.

Don Miguel called in his servant, spoke to her in a whisper and she departed. Moments later she returned with Judge Lunsford's court clerk in tow. Lunsford was clearly shocked. "I believe you gentlemen know each other," Don Miguel said, smiling. The smile faded and Don Miguel leaned forward toward Judge Lunsford. "You have taken my money and you have done far more than simply fail me." He pointed to the court clerk. "He has been on my personal payroll since my own trial and your every move, your every thought has come back to me."

"I . . ." Lunsford was suddenly frightened. He had a vision of his wife at the mercy of Juan and the others and of himself dying as he witnessed the atrocity, helpless to stop it.

Don Miguel motioned the servant and the court clerk out of the room. When the door closed, Miguel spoke again. "I am a man of infinite mercy, *señor*." He extended his hands in front of him, palms upward, "I understand the things that plague others and I wish only to help them with their troubles." The act nearly made Lunsford vomit but he dared not defy it. "Therefore, *amigo*, I am giving you this last chance. A clean slate with old troubles and bad feelings put behind us. A chance to show me that my judgment of you was justified."

Arlo Lunsford was visibly shaking and pale. He looked up. "What do you want me to do?"

"I have employed a gunman, the very best gunman money can buy. Today, he will dispatch this marshal, this man Morgan. Then, Judge, your slate will be clean again. When it is, you will make up tax papers on the properties on this list." Miguel handed Lunsford a paper. He started to look at it but Miguel stopped him. "You may read that when you return to your office. Your clerk will replace the real tax papers with the ones you draft and the sheriff will serve them to the owners."

"But taxes have been paid already. They will have receipts on their property showing them paid."

"Then you will hold a hearing, an appeal hearing and you will declare the receipts are forgeries." Miguel smiled. "We will acquire all of the land on which the Peralta treasure can be hidden, *mi amigo*." Lunsford swallowed. He had done many things already which were illegal but they were all easy to hide, easy to justify through blaming others. He had done nothing which could be traced to him directly. If he did this, he knew there would be no escape if the scheme failed.

"Now, *mi amigo*, let me explain one more thing to you. If you fail in this thing, you will lose all you have. Your fine home will go to me." Miguel smiled. "Your fine wife to Juan."

"I, uh, it will take some time," Lunsford said. "It isn't something I can do in a few days."

Don Miguel smiled and shook his head and said, "Of course not. Of course not. You think me a fool?" Lunsford shook his head. Miguel's smile disappeared. "You have one week, *señor*, one week."

The ride back to his home was the longest Judge Arlo Lunsford had ever endured. His head was swimming with what he'd been asked to do but even more, with the consequences of failure. There was something else in the back of Judge Lunsford's mind, however. Something which he believed even Don Miguel had not considered. What if Lee Morgan killed Carbona's hired gun? What then? Judge Lunsford began to calm himself down and by the time he reached home, he'd decided the last issue.

# 10

Morgan was less than five miles from Holtville when he caught the movement along the ridge to his right. He knew there was a rider up there and he'd suspected it for several miles. He decided if whoever was on his ass intended to act, they'd do it now. He opted not to wait.

At one point, the road was within fifty feet of the spiny ridge. Morgan would make his move at that juncture. He tensed himself for a sudden move as he approached the area but his thinking and effort proved needless. His pursuer had the same plan and made the move ahead of him, suddenly appearing in the road.

"Jeezus," Morgan mumbled. The rider was Felisa Marin. He rode straight up to her, carefully eyeing the terrain around him. He saw nothing but he still didn't like it. A man with a rifle up in those rocks had a clean shot at him now.

"I'm alone," she said, "and here to warn you." He considered her, remembering first, the warmth of her body. "Warn me about what?"

"Carbona has hired a man, a *pistolero*. He is already in town. He is supposed to kill you and then your young friends if necessary."

"That right," Morgan replied, still dubious. "Who is he?"

"Haskell," Felisa replied. "Does the name have meaning to you?"

Morgan looked down and then up again. "Yeah," he said, "it sure as hell does. It means the worst kind of trouble."

"Is he very fast, this Haskell?"

"Some say there's nobody around who's any faster." Felisa considered Morgan, herself remembering the warmth of his flesh and the gentleness of his touch. "And what do you say, Morgan?"

"I say you get back to your daddy and stay put."

"I can't," she said. "It is the other thing I have to warn you about." Morgan frowned. "My father has found something. Something new about the treasure. I'm not sure what it is but it has to do with Holtville."

"Shit!" Morgan thought a minute and then said, "Why can't you go back?"

"I stole it from his safe." She dipped into her ample cleavage and withdrew a carefully folded bit of old parchment paper. She gave it to Morgan. He quickly opened it and found it was a roughly drawn map of the center of Holtville. There were stains on the map which blotted out some of the old marks on it but two letters were clear, right in what was the center of town. The letters were M and C. Morgan looked up.

"No ideas as to what it means?" She shrugged. "Does he know you stole it?"

"Perhaps by now he does. If not, he soon will. When he discovers it missing, he will know it was me. No one else has the combination to the safe. He placed it in the safe in my bedroom. It was put there for my jewels, mine and Teresa's." She frowned. Morgan didn't need to hear the question.

"Teresa is fine. She is with Estralita Peralta and they are at the Lupton place. You go there too, now, fast." Felisa smiled and then moved her horse next to Morgan's. She leaned out of her own saddle and kissed him. "Come back," she said, "and Teresa and I will welcome you." Morgan felt a tug in his groin at the thought.

He watched her ride out of sight and then he rolled up the parchment into as small a roll as he could. Carefully, he stuffed it down into the barrel of his Winchester. He pulled the Colts and loaded the sixth chamber and then holstered it. He made two fast draws, flexing his grip around the butt and getting the feel of the weapon for a new day. Indeed, each day in the life of a gunman was one in which he must reassure himself of his skill. Yesterday's skills no longer counted and tomorrow's would only be put to the test if he survived today.

"Okay, Haskell, let's see if you're another John Ringo."

It was just after ten o'clock when Morgan rode into Holtville. There were not more than a dozen people on the main street and all but two of them scurried away when they saw him riding in. Three horses were tethered to the hitching rail in front of the Holtville Saloon. Morgan reined up there and dismounted. One of the men who hadn't fled was Cyrus Black of the *Holtville Courier.*

"Ty Prather and his lap dogs lit out before sunup. You got a reception committee waitin' for you, Morgan."

"Brock Haskell?"

Cy Black shook his head and said, "You ought to be a journalist, Morgan. I'm damned if you don't get information faster'n me. You know, a lot o' folks gave you up for dead 'til that meeting at the Lupton place. Now, the same ones are scared you'll stay alive and there'll be an all out war."

"That's a real familiar spot for me," Morgan said. "I'm damned if I do and damned if I don't," he grinned, "and I'm damned if I can figure out how I get into these spots."

"What's your plan?" Black looked at his watch. "If the stage is running on time, you've got about thirty-five minutes."

"My plan is real simple," Morgan said, "stay alive. Now I need a favor." Black looked at

Morgan quizzically.

"Name it, Morgan."

"The first chance you get, come get my rifle. Take it to your office and fish the paper out of the barrel."

"What?"

"Just do it," Morgan said. "After you've looked at the paper, do some research and find out all you can about it."

"And then what?"

"If my plan works, I'll be over to your office to hear what you found out. If it doesn't, see to it the information gets to Tad Winfrey. He and his sister will be in town today. If it works that way, there's one more thing you can do for me too."

"And what's that?"

"Send a telegraph to Los Angeles and explain what took place."

"Who do I send it to?"

"Wyatt Earp."

Morgan entered the saloon and took up a spot at the far end of the bar facing the batwing doors. There was no rear door. Two saloon girls were already plying their trade to the half a dozen men in the place. One card game was in progress and the barkeep was busy washing glasses.

"You drinkin'," the barkeep asked and then added, "Marshal?" Morgan glanced up. The barkeep was smiling.

"A beer." Morgan put out the money for it but the barkeep pushed it away. "Why so generous?"

"In about fifteen minutes, Marshal, there'll be more customers in here than I can handle." He pointed a finger, "An' most of 'em will be here to see you."

"You mean to see me get shot, don't you?"

The barkeep drew himself a beer. "I s'pose there's a few still bettin' that way but not most, not no more." Morgan considered the barkeep and the man reached down and produced a copy of the *Courier*. "Not since Cy Black put this story in his paper." Morgan glanced at the headline.

"Son of Famed Old Time Shootist in Holtville"

"Ain't you gonna read it?"

"I already know who I am," Morgan said. He sipped his beer and glanced toward the front door. One of the girls wiggled her way over to him.

"My name's Mandy," she said, "and if there's ever a time I can be of service to you, Marshal, just let me or Jack here know."

"I'll remember," Morgan said and then he turned and addressed himself again to the barkeep. "You mentioned bets. Just who the hell instigated that?"

Jack jabbed his own chest with his finger. "Not me, if that's what you're thinkin'." He pointed to the girl, "Not her neither or any o' the girls." Morgan finished his beer and the barkeep gestured toward the empty mug. Morgan shook his head. "It was Haskell himself."

"When?"

"Yesterday," Jack thought for a moment, " 'bout noon as I recollect." There was a big clock over the back bar. Jack turned and looked up at it. "Yeah, 'bout noon." The barkeep turned back. "He tol' folks to be back down here this morning at quarter to eleven and that they'd have drinks on the house and their money either won or lost by eleven-thirty." Morgan looked up at the clock. It was twenty minutes before eleven.

"Did Haskell say anything about when he'd be here?"

"Eleven o'clock sharp," Jack said, "right here." Jack was pointing to a table in the corner of the room near the front window. "Ya know, this'll be the only gunfight Holtville has ever had. Mostly them days are gone. Prob'ly never be another chance to see one." Jack, the barkeep, finished his own beer and then held up the paper. "You really Buckskin Frank Leslie's son?"

Morgan eyed the barkeep, then Mandy and then looked around the room. All eyes were upon him. He supposed it was a legitimate question, given the circumstances, and it probably deserved a legitimate answer. Nonetheless, Morgan didn't like it. These people were here to see a native gunfighter stand up against the offspring of a legend. It was of a hell of a lot more interest and excitement to them than the Peralta gold or the fact that their little town was about to be torn asunder by a war of greed. Morgan said,

"That's what the paper says."

Jack had been right. People began pouring into the saloon. The batwing doors never had a chance to come together. As they entered, they'd pause, look around and then stare at Morgan a moment. Outside, their womenfolk were lining both sides of the street. Jack began serving drinks. Once, he got near Morgan and said, "I haven't seen this much activity in Holtville since the Fourth of July 'bout four years back. John L. Sillivan came through an' put on a exhibition bout."

Morgan had never seen Brock Haskell in person but the pictures he'd seen left no doubt about him when he walked into the saloon. Morgan's thoughts leaped back in time to the Spade Bit and the little shootist known as Kid Curry. Haskell was a little bigger but dressed in a store bought suit and a derby.

"Morgan," Haskell said, nodding his head. Morgan eyed the man but didn't respond. "Like to buy you a drink before I kill you." Morgan thought, "The sonuvabitch even acts like Kid Curry." Morgan remembered again when he'd first met little Harvey Logan and worse, when he'd bedded Harvey Logan's woman. Morgan was never sure how Logan ended up with the Kid Curry handle but it was Kid Curry who came after Morgan, all the way back to Idaho. It was Kid Curry who taunted and challenged him. It was, finally, Harvey Logan who stood against Morgan's father and they killed each other in the cookhouse at the Spade Bit Ranch. To this day, Morgan never knew who'd drawn first. He wondered if there would be witnesses to today's event who would think back and ask themselves the same question.

Morgan moved toward Haskell's table and the murmuring in the room stopped. Only the sound of Morgan's bootheels on the plank board floor could be heard. He scooted a chair out and sat down. Jack, the barkeep, brought a bottle of whiskey and two glasses. Brock Haskell looked up at the clock and then at Morgan. He smiled and poured them both a drink.

"I admired your daddy a lot," Haskell finally said. "I think the writers don't do him justice."

"Maybe he doesn't deserve it."

Haskell frowned. He was clearly puzzled by Morgan's first words.

Haskell considered Lee Morgan for several moments and then said, "Why do you say that? He was one of the best that ever lived."

"He's dead. Tying a man you pull on is the same as him beating you. You're just as dead." Haskell downed his drink. Morgan pushed his away. A faint moan rippled through the room. The onlookers were starting to weigh their betting decisions.

"You refusing to drink with me, Morgan?"

Morgan got to his feet, glanced up at the clock and then back at Haskell. He raised the volume of his voice just a bit as he said, "I haven't always been given a choice about who I have to kill and who I don't but I still have the choice of who I drink with, Haskell, and on a list of two, you'd come in third." Morgan wheeled and walked toward the door.

"You're a dead man, Morgan," Haskell said. Morgan pushed through the batwings and walked into the street. Inside, Brock Haskell's face was flushed. The men he'd challenged before had always drank with him, except those few he'd hunted down outside of a town. Haskell always tried to have his gunfights in a town. A town with a newspaper and a populace which was perpetually bored by lack of excitement. Then and only then could Haskell perpetuate his own legend. It was a flaw in Brock Haskell and Morgan knew it. What he didn't know was whether or not it was enough of a flaw.

Morgan walked to the center of the street, turned to his right and walked another thirty feet. He turned around and let his eyes scan the crowd on both sides. Among the mostly women spectators there was a scattering of men. A few were just the old men of the town but most, perhaps eight or ten, Morgan reckoned, were riders for both Marin and Carbona. Cy Black was in the front row of one group. Morgan couldn't see Judge Arlo Lunsford. No one could. Lunsford was peering from a window a half a block distant and muttering a prayer to himself.

The batwings came open and Brock Haskell stepped out. He, too, paused and looked in both directions. He smiled. He was obviously pleased at the turnout. He glanced at the sky and made a mental note of the conditions. It would enhance the story when he told it and told it and retold it. The day he'd gunned down the famous Lee Morgan, then serving as a U.S. Marshal. Haskell walked to the middle of the street and turned to face Morgan. Someone shouted from behind him, "Stage is comin'."

Cy Black thought it odd that even the pigeons on the town's clock tower seemed frozen to their perches. He eyed the crowd and jotted down short descriptions of facial expressions and what people were doing with their hands. He also noted the men in the crowd with their clenched jaws, squinty eyes and dry lips.

Something, perhaps the increasingly louder sound of the stagecoach coming, frightened the pigeons. Their wings beat an uneven rhythm as they sought more suitable environs. A single feather was fluttering down, almost midway between Haskell and Morgan. Both men saw it and both had the same thought. When the feather struck the ground, it would be time for someone to die.

The feather floated slowly downward with a typical rocking motion. Back and forth, to and fro, four feet, three, two! Brock Haskell's arm made a sweep so sudden it was not possible to follow it.

Inexplicably, a breeze violated the otherwise deathly calm air. The feather rose a few inches and blew three feet closer to Brock Haskell. His eyes caught the movement. As a result, they missed Morgan's draw. By the time Haskell's eyes had raised again, he was staring into a puff of blue-gray smoke. His own pistol roared and he could see the steely expression on Lee Morgan's face change almost imperceptibly. Morgan winced. A fraction of a second later, Brock Haskell's expression changed. Haskell died.

"You're hit," Cy Black said to Morgan.

Morgan nodded and felt his right side just at his waist. His fingers traced the bloody crease left by Haskell's bullet.

The wiry little newspaperman kept the crowds away. He and Morgan watched four or five men mount up and ride, hell bent, out of town in both directions. Morgan got his mount and walked with Cy back to the office of the *Courier.* They had just stepped inside when the stage coach rattled by.

"I'd sure like to be in two places at once right now," Cy said, grinning. "Out at Marin's place and down at Carbona's." He turned back to Morgan. The two men smiled at one another and Cy nodded his head toward the back of the building. Morgan pushed aside the curtain and stepped into the back room of the *Courier.*

"G'mornin'," he said. Tad and Tammy Winfrey both hurried to him, Tad shaking his outstretched hand and Tammy stretching up to kiss his cheek.

"They got here just after midnight," Cy Black said, "just like you figured it."

# 11

Tammy Winfrey doctored Morgan's wound and wondered at how close a thing the gunfight had been. Already, however, the talk around town was how fast and sure Marshal Lee Morgan had been and that his bullet had passed, dead center, through Brock Haskell's heart.

After Tammy treated his wound, Morgan dressed in the buckskins he often wore if he planned to be on the trail. That done, he brought the Winfreys up to date on the events in and around Holtville since his arrival.

"And you've actually seen the pistol," Tammy asked after hearing Morgan's story about Lita Peralta. Morgan nodded. She looked at her brother. "Tad, my God, maybe it's almost over at last." He smiled, squeezed her hand and nodded.

"I don't want to throw cold water on your excitement," Morgan said, "but we still don't have the fourth grip and even if that map locates it for us, we can't just walk out of here with it. Marin and Carbona both will make a try for it and I have to remind you that we're just a little bit outgunned."

"Believe me, Morgan, I've thought of little else," Tad Winfrey said, "but I do have a surprise of my own for you." Morgan frowned. "We'll have to make a short ride but," he continued, pointing to Cy, "thanks to him, it's well hidden."

"No disrespect intended," Morgan said, "but I've had about all the surprises lately that I can stand."

Cy Black walked over to Morgan and slapped him on the arm. "Go with the lad, no questions asked, Morgan. This is one surprise you won't mind and I need a little time to check some things about this map." Morgan looked at each of the three and finally shrugged.

"Lead the way, Tad."

The way proved to be rather rough. North of Holtville, the terrain was increasingly difficult unless one stuck to the trail. Tad and Morgan did not. After four miles, Tad dismounted. Morgan followed suit and was eyeing the huge rocks and the narrow openings into them which seemed to disappear into nowhere.

"We go the last mile or so on foot. The horses won't make it. Indeed," Tad said, looking at

Morgan now and smiling, "the mules barely made it."

"Mules?" Tad smiled again and started walking. He motioned with his arm for Morgan to follow. Both men were perspiring when they finally reached the top of a ridge. Below was a cut between the rocks, accessible only by the route they'd taken or by a narrow and treacherous trail. Indeed, Morgan saw a team of six mules grazing at leisure. Tad started down. At the bottom, Morgan got his first look at the huge cave hewn from the stone by nature.

At the cave's mouth was a heavy wagon. Beneath the canvas cover, Morgan saw case upon case of dynamite. The back half of the wagon also contained a number of unmarked boxes.

"Where in the hell did you get this?" Morgan asked. "And what's in those?" He was pointing to one of the smaller boxes. Tad smiled and motioned to him. They went just inside the cave and Morgan saw another canvas tarp. Ted eyed him and Morgan walked over, undid one tie down and threw back the covering. "Jeezus!" He was staring down at a brand new Gatling gun.

"It won't win the war all by itself but it sure will even things up a little."

"A little?" Morgan grinned. "It's worth a whole damned battalion and it doesn't bleed or run." Morgan replaced the tarp and walked back to the wagon. "Ammunition?" Tad nodded. "Where?" Morgan said and then cut himself short, "on second thought, Tad, don't tell me, I don't want to know."

Tad frowned. "You don't?"

"You got it here, that's all I need to know."

"Thing is," Tad said, "it's a full day's work to get it out of here. I'll need some advance notice before it's moved."

"Yeah," Morgan agreed, "but the dynamite will buy that."

Joaquin Marin listened carefully to the report of his men. While Marin had nothing but contempt for Don Miguel, he had hoped Miguel's hired gun would eliminate this new and increasingly irritating thorn in his side. He had, on one or two occasions, entertained the idea of trying to convince Carbona to consider a pact between them but Joaquin Marin's whole being rebelled at the idea. He waved his men out of his presence and sat back to ponder his next move.

He had assumed he'd be hearing from Morgan. Marin still believed that Teresa had been taken by force and was being held until Morgan could get his money. Marin called his valet. "Wake Miss Marin," he said. The man looked odd. "Well?"

"She is gone, *señor*. She was gone early this morning." Marin couldn't believe his ears but when he realized the implications of the information, he leaped out of his chair and hurried to the bedroom. The safe was shut and locked and he felt a moment of relief. Once he had it open, the earlier anxiety turned into full fledged anger.

He'd been robbed by his own daughter. Now, Marin thought, he had no course of action left to him but one. If he was to find the pistol grip in Holtville, he would have to occupy Holtville, all of it.

"Order the men to assemble at once."

A mere half a day's ride away, Don Miguel Carbona was making his own plans. Certain that Lee Morgan was now just one more dead gunfighter, Carbona called in his top man. "I want you to put three dozen men into the countryside, a dozen in three groups. Ride to the surrounding farms and burn one or more of the outbuildings. I don't want you engaging in gun play. Shoot only in defense of yourselves. Make your attacks at night, hit and run."

"But I thought you were taking over the ranches with tax delinquencies?"

"I do not pay you to think," Carbona growled. "Your thinking right now only strengthens my resolve that I was right about you. I will take them over with tax delinquencies but I want their owners frightened and ready to give up."

"*Sí sí*, Don Miguel." The man turned to leave but quickly turned back. "What of Marin?"

Don Miguel looked up. "When I have taken over everything else, Marin will be surrounded. So will his water and supply line."

Carbona smiled. "It is the perfect military operation, the equivalent of the great campaigns of Santa Ana."

The man frowned. The only campaign of Santa Ana's that he could recall was originally launched against the Alamo, hardly a great military victory. He decided against mentioning it.

Tad Winfrey and Morgan arrived back at the office of the *Courier* to find an elated Cy Black. He was about to share his findings with Tammy when the two men arrived. They waited as he put the old parchment map on a table and next to it, some of the original land deeds and lot markers.

"Here," he said, pointing, "and here and here." He looked up. "All of that property was once marked off for private ownership but it was later deeded over to the citizens' council appointed by the Winfreys' father, Holt."

"Part of the original plat for the town," Morgan asked.

"Right. Now then, we have these letters, M and C." Morgan's eyebrows raised. "Damn," he said, "That's easy enough."

"It is when you're not thinking too much about other things and you've got the plat marked off. Marin and Carbona."

Tad Winfrey studied the map for a few moments and then looked up. All right, we have some land that was once owned by them and they gave it to our father, I'm still confused about their significance here."

"So was I," Cy said, "until I did a little more digging. There is one spot in this town, one and only one, where the land once owned by those two men have a common boundary. Two blocks from here at the corner where the general store is now located."

"You mean the letters show where the grip is buried?"

"Well, we might have to do a little assuming and use a little imagination but this map isn't of much value if that isn't the case."

"Who owns the general store?"

Cy Black jabbed a finger into the air, "As Shakespeare wrote, 'Aye, there's the rub.' Lester King bought it but he had to borrow against it. Later, the bank sold the note."

"To whom?"

Cy shrugged. "That, Morgan, I don't know."

The front door opened, Morgan's Bisley came up and Cy held up a hand and moved to the curtain. He peered out, turned around and said, "My God, it's Judge Lunsford." Cy stepped out front. "Judge, what can I do for you?" Cy thought the Judge looked pale and even frightened. He frowned. "Judge?"

"Lee Morgan," Lunsford said, "is he here?"

"Why?"

"Please, Black, I must see him, believe me, I must. It's a matter of life and death."

Cy Black didn't trust Lunsford and he glanced outside to see if there were any of Carbona's men visible. He saw nothing out of the ordinary but he was very cautious. "Whose life and death Judge?"

"Mine, Black, and that of my wife."

Cy led Judge Lunsford to the back room. In a few minutes, the judge explained what had happened to him that morning and the order he'd been given by Don Miguel Carbona.

"I can't," he slumped into a chair, "I won't do any more for him." The judge looked up. "I promised myself that I would fight against Carbona and Marin and everyone else if you killed that gunfighter. I need help but I also come with some to offer."

"Just why in the hell should we believe you, Judge," Morgan asked.

The judge nodded. "Yes, why? I asked myself that same question before I left my office." Judge Lunsford got to his feet and looked Morgan straight in the eye. "I knew that Prather and his cronies were out of town and couldn't follow me here but then there was my court clerk. He came back with me. What could I do?

"What did you do, Judge?" Morgan asked the question and moved over near the curtain where he could keep an eye on the front door.

"I made certain I wasn't followed and I got your proof for you at the same time. You see, I'm not a violent man."

"What certainty and what proof?" Cy asked.

Judge Lunsford swallowed. "My court clerk. You see, I killed him."

Morgan moved quickly to the judge's office and confirmed the judge's story. He was still somewhat skeptical, given that anyone could have killed the clerk. Nothing would make it easier for Carbona than to get a man on the side of his adversaries.

When Morgan got back to the office of the *Courier,* he found Judge Lunsford going over the plat maps and parchment. Morgan was none too happy about it.

"I found the clerk but it only proves he couldn't follow. I don't know if the judge killed him or not and I'm still not certain about his motives."

Cy Black listened and then said, "Morgan, he saw the plat and all the rest. He asked about it and I told him. After all, he's settled a number of boundary disputes. Most important, however, is the fact that he told us who ended up with the deed on the mercantile store."

"Who?"

"Me," Lunsford said, "I own it now or I will when Les King can't meet his bank payment."

"How many others like that one, Judge?"

"A drawer full, Morgan, but they'll all go back and be set straight if you'll help me. My wife must be protected. I'll take my own chances but I can help you, too."

"How's that?"

"Carbona gave me another chance. Let me capitalize on it for you. You give my wife protection and I'll keep him busy. I told you what he wants from me. Well, he wouldn't know a phony tax bill from the real thing. I'll just take him the real ones."

"Uh uh," Morgan said. "In the first place, you told him you'd need some time. Go back too soon and he's liable to get suspicious. Besides, there's still Prather and his deputies to deal with." Morgan moved across the room, looking down and pondering this latest turn of events. "There may be a way." He studied Judge Lunsford's face. "You'd be taking one helluva life threatening risk, Judge, if you're sincere."

"I told you what I want of you. Protection for my wife. Nothing more."

Cy Black stepped forward. "Morgan, if you're thinking what I think you're thinking."

"I am. The Peralta place. It would keep Carbona fairly well occupied for a few days. In that time we might just find what we're looking for."

Morgan explained to Judge Lunsford about the Peralta place and drew a crude map of how to get there. "Now you have your wife here by sundown tonight, We'll see to it she's safe."

Judge Arlo Lunsford went on his way and Morgan turned his attention back to the mercantile store. "We're going to pay a visit to Les King this evening," he said. "We can't afford to waste time observing the proprieties."

"Agreed, Morgan, but where do we start?"

"Let's get a look at what we've got to work with from the inside first, then we make that decision, Tad. In any event, you won't be along."

"What? Why not?"

"You're work is cut out for you. When Mrs. Lunsford arrives this evening, she'll be able to lead you to the Lupton place. You take her and Tammy here out there."

"That's tonight. What about tomorrow?"

"And I'm not staying out there when everything we're doing is here in town," Tammy said.

Morgan held up both hands. "You hired me

to do a job and Wyatt Earp told me to watch after both of you. You can fire me and then all I'll do is what Wyatt asked me to do but if you think I'm going to risk his being mad at me, you've got another think coming." Tammy smiled and shrugged. "As to tomorrow, Tad, you'll take what hands you need from the Lupton place and get our other treasures down out of those hills."

"The Gatling? But where do I bring it? The Lupton place?"

Morgan jabbed a finger at the floor. "Here," he said, "to Holtville. Whatever else we find, we'll find right here in town." He set his jaw and added, "And whatever fighting we end up having to do will be easiest done here. We've got a water supply, food, ammunition, a doctor, everything our enemies don't have, except men."

"It'll take most of the day," Tad said.

"Mebbe not. Take two wagons from the Lupton place. A tow horse team to go with them. Split the load on the one wagon between those two and use the mules to pull the Gatling on the big wagon."

"It'll work, sure it will," Tad said, excitedly. "We may have trouble getting those horses into that canyon though."

"You can bet on it but do it, Tad, and get on back here as fast as you can."

Cy Black returned to the back room. He looked grim. "Ty Prather and his deputies just rode in. You can be sure they'll ride right straight down to see the judge."

"Then it seems to me," Morgan said, "that they need a little distracting."

"Like what?"

"Put the word on the street that I'm looking for them, all three of 'em, and add that I'm none too damned happy with 'em."

Less than thirty minutes after Cy spread the word of Morgan's search for Ty Prather, Prather was gone. One of his deputies rode with him but the one they called Shorty did not. He was convinced that Morgan was no man at all without his guns and he decided he'd prove it. On top of that, if he could deliver Morgan to Carbona where the fast gun had failed, he'd be Carbona's new ramrod.

Shorty found circumstances working for him when he saw Morgan and Cy Black leave Cy's office. They got even better when he barged in on Tad and Tammy. Tad might have made a little more account of himself had he not been taken by surprise. As it was, Tad was soon unconscious and suffering a cracked jawbone.

Shorty eyed young Tammy Winfrey but his mind was much more on greed and power than on lust. He'd have her anyway, he thought to himself.

"You take care o' the kid there, girlie, and keep your mouth shut an' mebbe you won't git hurt." Tammy was scared but she did a commendable job of hiding it. She knelt down beside her brother and kept quiet.

Morgan and Cy Black fared little better in what they were supposed to be doing. Morgan decided that they couldn't wait until evening to talk to Les King at the mercantile store. They'd talk to him then and hopefully be able to make a search.

As Cy and Morgan approached the mercantile store, a rider came into town at full gallop. He reined up when he saw Lee Morgan and Morgan recognized him as one of the Lupton hands.

"Mizz Lupton sent me," he shouted, never bothering to dismount, "one of our boys on the south range saw 'em, Marin's men. They're comin', ridin' hard this way, comin' to Holtville."

"Damn!" Morgan had wanted to get the man off his horse, calmed down and speak to him privately. Now it was too late. Several bystanders heard the warning.

"Get down to the newspaper office," Morgan shouted. Three men approached. One of them looked angry.

"You brought this grief down on us, Marshal. We wasn't havin' no trouble with nobody 'til you come in." One of the others doubled up his fists and moved toward Cy Black. Morgan watched, open mouthed, as Cy threw up both his arms, danced backwards, sideways and then threw three quick punches at the man which broke his nose, split his lip and knocked him down, in that order.

"You get the hell in the saloon," Morgan told the second man, "and you round up every man that wants to fight. If you want to save your town, that's what you'll have to do. It's up to you." The man eyed his friend on the ground and then shook his head and ran off. Cy Black was already trotting off toward his office.

The Lupton hand dismounted and stood by the doorway waiting for Cy and Morgan. Morgan caught up with the little editor.

"That was a helluva demonstration back there, Cy." Cy looked over and smiled. "Lightweight champion pugilist in my college class," he said. They both looked up and the door to Cy's office opened behind the man who was waiting for them. Both expected to see Tad or Tammy.

"Look out," Cy shouted. Morgan stopped, drew and fired. Shorty's gun flew from his hand and he clutched at his chest, staggered and fell face down on the board sidewalk. Cy stopped.

"My God! That must be eighty feet or more." Morgan holstered the Bisley and the two men hurried on. Shorty was dead. Tammy told them what had happened after they left. Tad was up and around but in a lot of pain.

"We'll have to make some plan changes," Morgan told them, "and we'll have to do it damned fast. Marin's men are on their way. My guess is that they plan to take over Holtville."

Tad could speak only with considerable difficulty but he managed to ask, "How do we stop them? There's not time to get the Gatling."

"But there is time to fetch some of that dynamite," Morgan said. He quickly wrote out a note and handed it to Cy.

"You're going to have to miss a newspaper today, Cy. You're the only one that can ride back to the Lupton place. I need this man here and every other one I can round up in town plus any that can be spared from the ranch. Take Tad and Tammy with you."

"I've never missed a deadline, dammit! All I have to do is set the type."

"Cy, there's just not time."

"I can set type. I worked as an apprentice for two years." They both looked at Tammy. "I won't go to the Lupton place, Morgan, I'll just ride off the first chance I get and come right back here."

"Damn!" Morgan glanced at Cy. "Get going," he said, "we'll get the paper out one way or another." Cy and Tad rode off toward the Lupton place and Morgan turned to the ranch hand. "I saw you at the meeting that night but I don't know your name."

"Jake Ledbetter, Mr. Morgan, and I'm damned proud to be ridin' for ya."

"Mebbe right now, I'll ask again later. All right Jake, you get down to the saloon and organize every man there. I'll be joining you in a few minutes. I've got to go to the livery and fetch a wagon and team." Jake nodded and hurried off.

Inside, Tammy was already busying herself with the type tray. "You really do know what you're doing, don't you?" She stopped and looked up and smiled. "Did you think I'd lie just so I could stay in town?"

"The thought crossed my mind. You know there won't be anybody around to keep an eye on you for awhile. I will be leaving some men at the saloon but I don't want them to split up just yet. Too easy for Marin's men to slip in one at a time."

"Don't you worry about me, I'll be fine. As soon as the paper is run, I'll deliver it to the saloon. Folks can pick one up there. I'll stay there too." Tammy moved over to where Morgan stood. "Take care of yourself."

"Not much to worry about this trip. It's what happens afterwards that matters." Morgan looked at the clock. "We could be back by dark if we don't run into any real trouble." She pulled his face close to hers and kissed him. It was a soft, gentle kiss but it belonged to a woman, not a little girl. "I'll be waiting," she said.

Morgan freed some very frightened but very grateful people. He told them to go on home and stay there. The fight, he told them, was only about to begin. That done, he returned to the saloon. All eyes were on him when he walked through the batwing doors but only one person spoke up. Morgan knew him as Obie Grant, a local cattle rancher who harbored almost no use at all for guns or gunmen. His own son had fallen victim to a wet-nosed gunny a few years back.

"You're a damned loose man with other folk's lives, mister. Some here might think you're quite a hero but what you did was damn dumb. What if it hadn't worked?"

Morgan poured a drink, downed it, turned to Grant and said, "Then you wouldn't be asking me the question."

# 12

Morgan went straight to Arlo Lunsford's office. The judge had just finished packing the things he would need to resume his position on the bench at some future date. He'd also written a letter which highlighted those things in which he had become embroiled.

"Morgan? What is it?"

"I want a court order authorizing me to enter the sheriff's office and confiscate the weapons he keeps. Joaquin Marin's men are riding toward Holtville now to take it over or sack it."

"My God! Morgan, I . . . I can't issue an order like that." He handed Morgan the letter he'd written. Morgan read it, looked up and then tore the letter into pieces.

"Let's play out the hand we talked about today, Judge. You can always write that letter when things are over, if you still feel the need and you're still able. That court order is a helluva lot more important right now."

The judge looked down at the torn bits of paper and then shook his head. "Yes," he said, "you're right, Marshal, it is." He quickly penned the order and as he handed it to Morgan, he said, "What about my wife now?"

"Do you know the Lupton place?"

"Yes but I . . ."

"Cy Black will be there by the time you arrive. He'll get you in. Take your missus out there and you stay put too until you get word from me or someone." Lunsford nodded and Morgan turned to leave.

"Marshal." Morgan turned back. "I owe you, sir. I've been a fool. I hope I'm not too late in recognizing it."

"It's easy to tell when it's too late, Judge." Lunsford looked quizzical. Morgan smiled and said, "You're not breathing anymore."

Jake Ledbetter had rounded up eighteen men by the time Morgan arrived. Some were skeptical about what they'd heard but most of them knew Jake and trusted him. Morgan climbed up on a table. "You're all deputized as of this moment." He pointed to three men in front. "You three go on over to the sheriff's office, break in and bring every weapon and all the ammunition you can find. I have a court order approving it and I'm acting in an official capacity. Bring back any tin stars you find, too. You boys lay claim to the first three you find."

The official sanctions made all the difference to all the men. Certainly none of them had reason to question Morgan's cool head or courage or speed or accuracy. They had a leader.

While the three men went after the weapons, Morgan sent Jake to roust Les King, the mercantile owner. Morgan was also going to confiscate whatever King had in stock which could help defend the town. While those men were so engaged, he addressed the others.

"Jake will be in charge. I want six men with me." He looked around. "I want the best shots left here and the best arm wrestlers with me. I need strong backs. I want three men to ride south toward the Marin's spread. I want to know where Marin is and how fast he's moving. As soon as you spot him, send one rider back with the news and a second back half way. The first will keep an eye on their movement and report to the second who will ride back to town again. Keep the relay working until we don't need it anymore."

"Where you an' your men gonna be, Marshal?" Morgan considered the man who'd asked the question. The tone of his voice indicated he didn't think much of a leader who was riding away from his men right off. Morgan saw the man was big, broad shouldered and with meaty, muscular arms.

"Tell you what," Morgan said, "I accept

your question as a commitment that you've volunteered to ride with me. I can use your brawn and you can use your brain to get the answer to your question first hand." The others broke into laughter.

Cy Black and Tad Winfrey had stayed to the dry washes which scored the landscape south of Holtville and out toward the Lupton ranch. By dusk however, they moved closer to the trail and by full dark, they were moving through the low, undulating hills which rolled into Lupton valley.

"Cy, look there, off to the southwest." Both men reined up. There was a red-orange glow in the sky. It appeared almost as a second sunset. "What is it?"

Cy Black knew what it was at once. He'd seen it before, many times and much worse. "Fire," he said. "Could be prairie or could be buildings but it's a fire sure. I saw more than I wanted to up north. Forest fires. A few big prairie fires, too, back when the Indians were still active."

"Don't strike me as being a lot of things on this particular prairie that would burn that big," Tad said.

"You're right, Tad, there isn't. Let's move faster."

Cy and Tad were not the only witnesses to the blaze. Joaquin Marin had opted to lead his own men to Holtville once he'd learned of his daughter's treachery. Now his point rider returned to the main body and Marin halted his gang. He had more than sixty men riding in, more than enough as far as he was concerned to either take Holtville or destroy it.

"It's a fire, sizeable," Marin said, "but where?"

"I place it around *señor* Thomas's ranch," the point man said. Marin considered the opinion a moment and then concurred. "Yes, that would be about right. Thomas has a huge barn but nothing else would make such a large blaze unless. . . ." he stopped himself. He watched the blaze for a few moments more and then snapped out a new order. "I want one more drag rider, two more men on the flanks." He looked at the point rider. "Keep a sharp watch, slow the pace just slightly and watch for more such signs of a fire." The man looked puzzled but he nodded.

Marin had originally planned to take Holtville that very night. Now, he opted to wait it out until morning. He wanted a looksee at the town before he made his move and if everything looked normal, he would simply ride in at dawn and have it before anyone could muster resistance. He looked at his pocket watch. At the new pace he'd chosen, his men would have about three hours to rest after they reached Holtville's outskirts. Once again he turned and looked toward the glow in the sky. He had a sinking feeling in the pit of his stomach. He clearly felt that something was wrong, something which spelled trouble for him but he couldn't stop his plan on that alone.

Less than an hour later, the point rider rejoined the main body again. There was a second and third fire now visible.

"Carbona *Bastardo!*" In Spanish, Marin ordered a patrol of six men to ride to the nearest of the blazes and confirm his suspicions. He also ordered a closing of his own ranks. He did want to maintain the pace he'd set however.

"We cannot," he told his point man, "afford to ride into Holtville after dawn."

Joaquin Marin was not the only man with decisions to be made and little time in which to make them. Only thirty minutes before his first arson patrol had struck, Miguel Carbona's men rode in from Holtville.

He knew they looked grim when they entered his study. He wrinkled his nose at the roady odor and dirty appearance. "Well?" None of the men wanted to act as the spokesman. Spanish history abounded with tales of the messenger who had paid with his life for the message he carried. Carbona looked at each face and he got his answer. "Was it a fair fight? A stand up fight between Morgan and Haskell?"

"*Sí.*" It was all any of them could manage.

Don Miguel waved the men out of his presence and poured himself a healthy quantity of tequila. He downed it and then sat down to ponder his problem and its most likely solution. He would not be stopped by a lone *Yanqui pistolero.*

The most accurate information about the

origin of the fires in the early evening sky was even then coming into the Lupton ranch. Half a dozen families had already arrived and were telling of the marauders who had ridden down on them, screaming, shooting and burning. Carbona's men had liquored themselves up before they ever took to the countryside and the fire they'd been ordered to set became only the climax of their raids.

One family reported the deaths of their three hired men, the theft of their stock and their own near brush with death. Those with young girls in their families were the most fearful and the night of terror was only beginning.

Mary Lupton gathered her foreman and the three women together as more fires were spotted and more families arrived.

"I'm ashamed to have to ask you this but we must know." She was looking at the Marin sisters and it was the recently arrived Felisa who responded.

"Is my father responsible for these fires and this horror?" She looked down, she glanced at her sister and then at Lita. Finally she looked back at Mary Lupton. "Do not be ashamed to ask such a thing. My shame is in the fact that I cannot give you an answer, I don't know. I do know that he is capable of it and I fear that he and Carbona may join forces."

"That has been my fear as well," Mary said, "but it seems both men are driven by a personal greed that has, so far, worked to our advantage."

Lita Peralta stepped forward. Mary Lupton saw the tears in her eyes. Mary started to speak but Lita held up her hand and then the oilcloth wrapping.

"This," she said, "is the cause of the trouble. When this began, I believed in the system of justice. I believed what was rightfully mine would be restored to me and that my family name would again have real meaning in California." She threw the pistol on the floor. "Instead, it has brought out the worst in men and now claims the lives and homes of innocent people. The very peons I'd one day hoped to help with the treasure. We must give up the fight. Let them have the gun and the gold."

Cho Ping entered the room. "Two riders come. Men. They come from the north."

Teresa turned. "Morgan," she said, softly.

The two riders proved to be Cy Black and Tad Winfred. They were ushered at once into the house. Mary Lupton began the introductions. They were halted when Tad and Lita met.

"I feel I have a family again," Lita said. She hugged Tad, gently touching his swollen jaw and kissing his cheek.

"I hate to put a damper on a family reunion," Cy said, "but we have some very real and immediate dangers to deal with." Mary Lupton quickly brought the two men up to date on the events of the past couple of hours. In turn, Cy Black told the gathering what had occurred in Holtville and what Morgan was planning to do about it.

"Lita wants to end it," Mary said. "She believes the Peralta gold is at fault."

"The Peralta curse," Lita said, "has become the reality. The Peralta gold remains only a legend." She turned to Tad. "Will you and your sister give up your claims so that we might end the bloodshed?''

"Whoa there, little lady," Cy Black said, "just hold on. The sincerity of your offer is above reproach. Of that, I'm certain. It's practical application is foolhardy." Tad Winfrey seemed to take umbrage with Cy's assessment and was about to say so. The newspaperman smiled, understandingly, at Tad. "These men won't stop." He looked at the Marin sisters. "Your father? You know him better than any of us? Would he stop driving people from their homes, taking their land and their pride if he had the treasure?''

Tad Winfrey was shocked. "Damn you, Black, that's the most crude and painful thing I've ever seen done in my life."

"You may well be right," Cy said, still looking at the Marin girls, "but the issue here is the truth of the words, not the grace with which they were spoken."

Felisa Marin responded but she addressed herself not to Cy Black or Tad Winfrey but to Estralita Peralta.

"*Señor* Black is quite correct," she began. "Our father and Don Miguel Carbona will not be stopped by giving them the gold, they will only become worse. They lust after power, not gold. They seek gold only because they know it will buy more power. You may give them the pistols and they may find the treasure but after that, they will only want more. Always," she said, her voice cracking with emotion, "always they will seek more power over lesser men. I know of only one thing which will stop our father."

"What then," Tad asked.

"His death!" Tad was sorry he'd asked.

Cy Black gave the moment only the time he felt they could afford. It wasn't much. "We've got to get these families organized and ready to move out of here. Holtville is our only chance and we can't wait beyond midnight to leave."

"I know most of these people," Mary Lupton said. "I'll inform them and my men can help ready them for the trip. I can use your help, girls." They nodded and the women took their leave.

"Cy," Tad said, "I'm sorry I shot off at you that way."

Cy smiled and slapped Tad on the arm. "Youth and pretty girls and their defense against old men with sharp tongues goes back several thousand years. No need to apologize for that." Tad's face flushed and he grinned. "By the by, how's the jaw?"

"Painful but if I keep busy, I don't think about it, so I'd like to keep busy. Someone needs to ride out of here, right now, back to Holtville. Morgan ought to know we're on our way and there may be some men available to come out a ways and escort these people, just in case."

"Are you volunteering?"

"No, Cy, I'm telling you that's what I'm going to do."

"Yeah, that's kind of what I thought. Watch yourself, son." Tad nodded.

# 13

If things had not gone well up to that time for Morgan, he couldn't quarrel with his latest efforts and plans. By midnight, only the Gatling gun was not yet in Holtville but it was on its way. The movement of the ammunition for the wonder gun and the transport of the dynamite had gone without a hitch.

Les King was also a Godsend. He had just received a huge dynamite shipment himself, to be used to clear land. Too, he had an inventory of twenty-five rifles and thirty-two handguns and plenty of ammunition.

Morgan found Jake Ledbetter to be an efficient man to leave in charge and by the time Morgan had returned from the hidden canyon, Jake had rounded up nearly forty men. He was using two dozen of them in a hastily conceived defense perimeter at the south edge of town.

"From the looks of the fires to the south, I'm betting that we won't get hit 'til sunup. By then," Morgan told Jake, "we'll have a few more surprises in store for our visitors."

"What have you got in mind?"

"Something to eat and a little sleep," Morgan said, "and I'd suggest the same for every man we can spare. Change the perimeter so that those men can get a break, too, and catch some shuteye yourself." Jake nodded. "I'll be back at three."

Morgan couldn't remember the last time he was so damn tired. He ached in every muscle and joint and his stomach must have believed that his throat had been cut. He wolfed down a steak, some boiled potatoes, two pieces of apple pie and a quart of milk. It was one-thirty when he got back to the newspaper office. He found a fresh pot of coffee and he took a few more minutes of relaxation with a cup of it and a cigar.

Cy Black kept a small cot in the back and Morgan didn't bother with a light. He slipped into the office, stripped off his boots, shirt and pants and started to climb in.

"I'm glad you're back," Tammy said.

"Goddam, I didn't know you were in here. You're supposed to be in a room at the hotel.."

"But I'm not." Tammy raised up on her arms and the thin sheet slipped lower. Morgan could see the pink top edges of her nipples and the little protrusions indicating their hardness.

"Dammit, Tammy!" Morgan pushed away from her and stood up. "I'll go to the hotel."

She swung her legs to the floor, stood up and let the sheet drop away. The body was young, firm, shapely and the fleecy, golden patch between her thighs revealed her most private asset.

"Don't you want me, Morgan?"

"It wouldn't make a goddam bit of difference if I did."

"Do you think I'm too young? Is that it?"

"I know how old you are," Morgan said, fumbling for the sheet so that he might cover her.

"Then it's my uncle, Wyatt Earp?" She giggled. "Surely you're not afraid of Tad." Morgan took the edges of the sheet, reached behind Tammy and started to drape the sheet over her shoulders. She grabbed his wrists, jerked and then put his open palms against her breasts. At the same time, she stepped forward and pressed against him.

Morgan backed up but Tammy moved with him, all the way to the wall. She stood on her tip toes and locked her fingers around the back of his neck. She pressed tightly against him and, in spite of himself, Morgan reacted.

"I am my own woman," she said, softly. "I don't answer to my brother or to my uncle."

"And I'm a damned fool," Morgan said. He pushed Tammy back to the bed and mounted her. He found himself wanting to be inside of her. Morgan liked to take it slow and easy with a woman, working up to a mutual moment of gratification. Now, here with Tammy, he felt an almost animal lust. He wriggled out of his under drawers and was not surprised to find her moist enough to accommodate him at once.

"Yes," she whispered, "Oh Morgan, yes. Take me."

The initial thrust by Morgan was met with Tammy's undulating hips but they soon dropped into a pleasure filled rhythm. Tammy's youth resulted in additional pleasure for Morgan and he didn't want it to end too quickly. He gradually slowed and then stopped his strokes. He pulled out of her and began bathing her body with his lips and tongue.

Tammy writhed and moaned and whispered her adoration of his efforts. Her only two previous experiences had been with boys. Lee Morgan was a man and he was treating her like a woman. While her mind may not yet have reached that stage, her physical attributes and needs both belied the fact.

Tammy felt new feelings and experienced new sensations as Morgan fondled, stroked, teased and mouthed her. Twice she experienced total fulfillment and learned that she was capable of even more. Morgan wanted no more from her than what she had already offered, herself, completely. Having more than satisfied her desires, Morgan now entered her again and fulfilled his own needs. Both were spent and they fell asleep entwined in total satisfaction.

Morgan's internal alarm didn't have a chance to function on this morning. Jake Ledbetter awakened him, virtually ignoring Tammy Winfrey's presence. Morgan sat up. Jake was holding a lamp.

"Get that damned thing out of my eyes," Morgan said. He got up and started pulling on his britches. "Sorry Jake." Jake stepped back. "What's wrong?"

Jake looked down now at Tammy. She appeared to be asleep. "Her brother just rode in. He's over at the saloon."

Morgan considered Jake and said, "Why'd he come back?"

Jake told Morgan as much as he knew and then added, "But I just found out we've got worse problems."

Morgan tucked in his shirt and then sat down and began pulling on his boots. "Like what?"

"The sheriff."

Morgan frowned. "Prather? What the hell problem is Prather? Hell, he rode out of here hours ago and I'd be damned surprised if he ever came back."

"Be surprised, Morgan." Tammy woke up, rubbed her eyes, turned over and sat up. She was bare breasted and grabbed for a blanket when she finally saw Jake. He smiled, sheepishly.

"Jake, dammit!"

Jake Ledbetter set the lamp on the table. He stood for a moment and then took a deep breath and said, "I didn't tell the men I posted about

Prather. Most still take 'im for a lawman. He came back, Morgan, with fifteen men. He's holed up in the stock stable down by the courthouse."

Morgan turned to Tammy. "Get dressed and go over to the saloon. Tad's there." She glanced at Jake and then nodded. "All right, so Prather thinks he can buffalo us with fifteen men. Hell, we'll blow him out of the damned place, if we have to."

Jake swallowed. "He's got Howard Tuck an' his wife an' little girl in there, Morgan. Tuck's the town banker. He tricked 'em into going with 'im. Now he's got 'em up in the loft with ropes around their necks. Threatens to push 'em off unless we give 'im what he wants."

"Which is?"

"You, Morgan, dead!"

Jake had trouble keeping up with Morgan as they hurried off to the saloon. When they got there, Morgan stopped just outside. "Do they know?" he asked, pointing inside.

"They know and most won't listen to too much. They all owe Tuck an' he's their friend. You're still a stranger to 'em. They'll fight with ya but when it comes to a choice between you an' one o' their own, it's no contest, badge or no badge."

Morgan smiled. "Why do you think I hate badges so much."

Morgan pushed his way inside. He spotted Tad and walked over to him. "What time did Cy figure to pull out of the Lupton place?"

"Midnight. They'll be pushed hard to beat

daylight."

"Jake," Morgan said, "you ride out, north."

"The Gatling?" Morgan nodded. "I'll git back as soon as I can." Jake set his jaw and then added, "Stay alive, Morgan. This town needs ya whether these folks know it or not." Jake pulled out and Tad Winfrey poured he and Morgan a drink and gestured with his eyes toward the men in the saloon.

"They're getting mighty edgy. What now?" He downed his own drink and watched Morgan slosh his around in the glass for a minute. Finally, Morgan downed it.

"I'll be back in a few minutes." Morgan passed Tammy at the batwings. They looked at each other and exchanged the faintest of smiles. Tammy hurried over to join Tad but Morgan was already near the end of the block. He drew the Bisley and fired into the air, twice.

Everyone in the saloon came out onto the street. They could see Morgan's silhouette but nothing in the barn. The only evidence of anyone was the exchange of dialogue and the men all recognized the high pitched squeak belonging to Ty Prather.

"Well if it ain't the big shot marshal with the real sudden gun. Now then, Mr. Big Shot Marshal, if you're ready to strike a bargain, ol' Sheriff Prather'll tell you what to do."

"I'm not interested in what you've got to say, Prather. I don't know why you think I'm in Holtville but let me set it straight right now. I came here for gold and I don't give a damn about anything or anybody else. I just came up here to warn you. If you get in my way, I'll kill you."

Ty Prather was peering between two rotten boards and he could see Morgan holster his gun, turn around and start walking away. He shouted, "Morgan! You walk away from me an' I'll hang these folks." He waited but Morgan kept walking. "Morgan, goddam you, I'll do it, I'll hang 'em, I swear it."

Morgan was looking straight ahead. The shock hadn't worn off yet and the men were frozen in awe. Morgan knew that once they realized he wasn't bluffing, they'd probably do something very stupid. He hoped he had enough time to prevent the situation from ever getting that far.

"Morgan! Here I am. I'll do it. I'll hang this goddam banker." Morgan had been able to see the Tucks fairly well. Indeed they were tied into chairs and he'd noted they were also gagged. He was grateful for that. Had there been screaming he didn't know if he would have been able to hold back the townsmen.

Morgan stopped and turned around. Now he could see Prather framed in the barn's loft door. He gauged the distance.

I'm tired of listening to you, Prather," Morgan shouted. "You're not going to hang these folks, one of your men will have to do that and after they do, I'll blow that barn all to hell. It was the first building we set with dynamite. The very first one. You're a real smart man."

"Your goddamn bluffin' won't wash with

me, Morgan. You're a mighty good man with a handgun but you can't out fox ol' Ty Prather." Prather stepped next to the chair of banker Tuck. "He'll be first an' just why the hell do you figger one o' my men'll hang 'em, 'stead of me?"

"I already told you that, Prather," Morgan said. He'd gauged the distance at about forty yards. "I told you, I'm tired of listening to you."

"So what?"

"Because I consider a man I'm tired of as a man who's in my way." Morgan drew and let his arm make a stiff arc until the gun barrel was at a forty-five degree angle and then he squeezed the trigger. No one who witnessed the shot could believe it, particularly Holtville Sheriff Ty Prather. In an instant, he became Holtville's late Sheriff, Ty Prather.

Morgan fired two more shots into the side of the barn. He placed them where he'd seen shadows of men. He hit no one.

He knew it didn't matter. He'd hit Ty Prather. The sheriff had just hit the ground. If Morgan's bullet didn't kill him, the fall did. He broke his neck. Morgan detected no movement inside the barn. He made his next move.

"Anybody else in there who thinks I'm bluffing, go on and move up to the loft and hang those folks. After you do, I'll keep my promise to you just like I kept it to the little weasel you were riding with. I'll blow that building all to hell."

Morgan was very curious about the quality of the men in that barn. Where the hell had

Prather come up with them? They weren't Carbona's men, that was sure. Had that been the case, one of them would have taken a shot at him, perhaps more than one. He was certain they were armed with rifles, or some of them anyway. He concluded they were mostly out of work drovers that Prather had enticed into the deal with the promise of some big payoff. Now, they were leaderless.

"If you're not going to hang those folks, then I'd suggest you get the hell out of that barn, right now!" A few moments later, Morgan did hear movement. Horses! There were only two or three at first, then many more. All of them were at the back of the building and moving fast, away from town. Morgan waited. After five minutes, he strolled into the barn.

# 14

Jake Ledbetter came through the batwing doors of the saloon and looked around. His eyebrows raised. He was impressed. He sought out Lee Morgan in the back office.

"You've done a helluva job out there," he said. "The place looks like an army headquarters."

Morgan was looking over a supply inventory which one of the women had just completed. He finished, looked up and smiled.

"If we're going to stay alive and save this town, that's the way it will have to function."

"The Gatling gun is in place and rigged just the way you ordered it. I'll, by God, say one thing. Those Amish folk might not fight but, I swan, they can build anything."

"The sharpshooters in position?"

Jake nodded. "I've got two on each side of town. There are a dozen more men who rank close to the first eight. I got four o' them on the roof of the courthouse, two with the Gatlin gun and the rest for replacements."

"Yeah, good, Jake, good." Morgan got up, pulled his shoulders back and worked his arms up and down to limber up the stiff and tired muscles. "The women will divide the duty here. Hot coffee, food, medical treatment as the doctor dictates it. Now, how about the dynamite?"

"Two lines of it buried about a quarter of a mile out and another line about a hundred and fifty yards from the outside defense ring. That'll cover us on the southwest and the southeast quadrant."

Morgan reached out and slapped Jake on the arm. "You've done a helluva fine job yourself, Jake. It's a pleasure knowing you and I hope we can get drunk together tonight."

"I'm countin' on it."

"Well, there's no damned reason we can't start the day off right, is there?"

Jake grinned. "Not a damned one I can think of, Morgan."

Down the block, Cy Black finished setting the type for the day's paper. There were two headlines and two sets of type for the main story.

190

The first read,

>Holtville, California Sacked
>and Burned By Marauders

Cy smiled and picked up the second lead plate. He gently kissed the top of it. "You're the one. You've just got to be."

>Bloodthirsty Marauders Meet Their Doom
>Holtville, California Their Waterloo

Cy placed both plates in his safe and shut and locked it.

Some ninety men were now in the confines of the town's buildings. Of that number, a dozen were too old to fight and eighteen more were of the Amish persuasion. Fifty-three were fully armed and considered the town's front line of defense. Five others, all with army experience, were in the field to watch for and report on the movement of either the raiders of Joaquin Marin or the small Mexican terrorist army of Don Miguel Carbona.

In fact, many of Carbona's men were sleeping off a night of too much tequila and too many *señoritas*. Carbona himself was waiting reports from the men he'd sent out the night before to burn buildings and put fear into the hearts of the ranchers. What they had succeeded in doing was to strengthen an already steely resolve.

While Carbona waited, Joaquin Marin

paced. His main body of men was still a hard two hour ride away from Holtville, and he didn't want to move until the patrols he'd sent out returned. He was irritated, too, by the fact that he'd sent out similar patrols the night before to bring him news of the many fires which had been seen. He'd heard nothing from any of them.

Unknown to either side, except by the participants, all but two of Carbona's raiders were dead. Half drunk and all crazy, they had run headlong into Marin's sober and prepared men.

The fight was short and one-sided but Marin's men did not escape unscathed. Forced from their mounts to fight in a skirmish line, their animals bolted and left them afoot. Indeed, the gods had made light of the mortals on this night and they were about to deliver their final, ironic touch.

Don Miguel Carbona was more than a little surprised to find he had an early morning visitor. When Judge Arlo Lunsford was ushered into his presence, Miguel gave him a long, studied look. He did not offer his usual greeting or gesture to a chair. Lunsford remained standing, holding a thick, official looking folder.

"I did not expect to see you very soon, my dear Judge."

"Nor I you, Don Miguel, but if we are to reconcile our misunderstandings and gain an ultimate victory, then we must move quickly. I saw fires on the horizon last night. I wondered if you did."

"I ordered them." Miguel said, calmly. "The

combination of fear and fact is often too much of an obstacle for the peon, whether American or Mexican. I have now provided the fear."

"And the facts, as you choose to call them, are here." Lunsford hugged the folder to him and touched it lightly.

"The taxes?" Miguel asked, leaning forward.

"Yes," Lunsford said and then invited himself to sit down. Miguel's smile faded. He leaned back and glanced at the big floor clock.

"You must have worked very diligently and very, very late to have had such sudden success." Miguel got up and walked around his desk, sitting then on its edge. "And you must have ridden out of Holtville very, very early to have arrived here at this hour."

"The important thing, Don Miguel, is not that I am here, but why." Judge Lunsford now launched into one the finer moments of his later years. He tossed the tax folder on Miguel's desk with an air of total disinterest. Now, he leaned forward. "I know where Estralita Peralta is, and I know the locations of all four pistol grips." Arlo Lunsford smiled. It was a smug look he gave Carbona and it did not go begging.

"You speak as though you have brought me more than what we had originally bargained for, my dear Judge." Carbona turned icy. "You have not. Even if what you say is true, it is no more than what you promised and some of it is long overdue."

"Indeed it is, Don Miguel, but the last part,

the last pistol grip, that isn't overdue and it is worth considerably more than merely clearing my obligation to you."

"I will not be blackmailed," Miguel shouted. Two *vaqueros* entered the room and looked at Carbona, awaiting their orders. Judge Lunsford smiled, leaned back in the chair and folded his arms.

"Are you going to order me shot then, Miguel?"

The big Mexican bandit had never been in quite this spot. He finally waved his two men away.

"What is it you want?"

"One third of the Peralta treasure." Miguel's jaw dropped. He was stunned by the request. Judge Lunsford let Carbona's stew reach a simmer and then he continued. "I will take you to the Peralta woman's hiding place. There, we will find one of the pistols." Lunsford stopped talking and Miguel Carbona couldn't stand it.

"Then what?"

"One step at a time, Carbona." Lunsford never addressed Don Miguel in such a fashion. It rendered him an equal by Carbona's tradition and he didn't accept it. He was miffed, angry and frustrated all at the same time.

"When do we go?"

"We don't," Lunsford said. "If we go there first, we may miss our chance at the other two grips." Judge Lunsford calmly got to his feet and walked to Carbona's liquor cabinet.

"A drink, Don Miguel?" The wily judge smiled when he asked the question but he also realized that he had pushed Carbona about as far as any man could. When he received no reply, Judge Lunsford shrugged, poured himself a shot of Carbona's treasured bourbon, downed it and then turned around. "Joaquin Marin will attack Holtville this morning. He intends to take it over or destroy it. If he does either one, we could lose our chance at the Peralta gold for good."

"You come with much talk, Judge Lunsford," Don Miguel said, picking up the folder, "and legal papers which you told me would take a week to produce." He threw the folder down. "Now you wish to share a third of the wealth which has been due to me for centuries." Carbona suddenly drew a pistol and cocked it. He held it at arm's length and pointed it at Judge Lunsford's head. "I could have killed you before for your lies but I was gracious to you. Now you come into my home, insult my intelligence with more lies and try to rob me with your words."

Arlo Lunsford had not played such a game with a man since his days as a young attorney in the court room of Ohio. He knew Carbona to be so volatile a man at times, that he would kill even if it meant losing the treasure. Lunsford was on very thin ice. He thought, *It's prima facie time.*

"We waste time, Don Miguel. I ride with you. If I'm lying, kill me then." Miguel straightened, steadied the pistol and took two steps toward the Judge. Lunsford suspected what was next.

"Where is Luis?" There it was, the key question! Luis, the court clerk, faithful to Don Miguel. His eyes and ears in Lunsford's life. Luis, the Judge's prima facie evidence.

"He is dead, Don Miguel. I killed him myself. I have suspected him for as long as you have suspected me. I told him what I had learned and his actions were predictable. He checked my story and my information and then he rode straight to Marin. I had him followed. When he returned, I killed him and came here."

Lunsford was counting on a number of things to work in his favor where Carbona was concerned but the shock effect of his story about Luis and the lack of time were his most potent allies. Now, he'd used them both. The first sign of Carbona's reaction was the pistol barrel. It wavered and then slowly came down. The second was Carbona's one, almost whispered response. "Luis, Luis."

Judge Arlo Lunsford had not killed the court clerk merely to remove an obstacle. The judge had also learned a truth. Luis was, in fact, Luis Manuel Carbona, Don Miguel's brother.

Judge Arlo Lunsford had found his own treasure. He'd lost it years before but now he had it back and he was bent on never losing it again. What he found was himself. While taking his wife to the Lupton place, they had met the people fleeing toward town and Lunsford then learned of Marin's plan. By the time Lunsford reached Carbona, he'd altered the plan he and

Morgan had worked out. Lunsford would not simply lead Carbona on a wild goose chase. He would attempt to pit Carbona and Marin against each other in a pitch battle. Let them destroy or at least weaken their forces and give the citizens in Holtville a fighting chance.

Don Miguel Carbona, resplendent in his black and silver garb and mounted upon a white stallion, personally led the first charge against Joaquin Marin's encampment. Carbona was beside himself with anger at his own lieutenants for their treachery and disobedience of the previous night but it was easy to stifle such feelings at this moment.

Marin was caught totally by surprise and suffered heavy losses before his own men could find suitable ground on which to make a stand. In Marin's favor was the fact that Carbona's men were scattered and by the time he could gather his entire force, Marin was prepared. Holtville, for the moment, got a reprieve.

In Holtville, Lee Morgan sequestered himself with Cy Black, the Winfreys, the Marin girls and Lita Peralta. They waited. They had talked, chattered as much as anything, during the last hour before sunup but their talk ran out and they busied themselves with their own thoughts now. Sunup came but the imminent attack from Joaquin Marin did not. Two hours past sunup, the attack had still not come. What did come was one of the patrol riders Jake Ledbetter had sent south to track Marin.

Jack burst into the office at the saloon and Morgan was on his feet in an instant. The others followed suit. Jake had been waiting for his man and was the first to get the news. He was grinning from ear to ear.

"How the hell it happened I don't know. Why, I don't know but Carbona and Marin are at war, all out, winner take all war!" He gave the little gathering the report he'd gotten from his man and a cheer went up. They danced around, hugged one another and would not have stopped save for Morgan.

"We've got a cheer or two coming," he finally said, "but we're a helluva ways from an all out *fiesta, amigos*." Stern looks replaced the smiles when the reality of Morgan's observation soaked in.

Cy Black said, "You're right, of course. Can we exploit this?"

Morgan walked across the room, pondering the news and considering every possibility and each alternative to them. He stopped and turned to Jake. "A decoy! We need a damned decoy."

"I don't follow," Jake said.

"Look, neither Carbona or Marin want to die. They want the Peralta treasure. One or both of them is going to come to his senses before they've killed each other off. We're going to be facing whatever is left. A hundred men, fifty? Hell, I don't know and the worst possible scenario is, in fact, a peace and an agreement between them. We have to split up whatever is left."

Cy Black smiled. "Divide the enemy force and destroy the halves piecemeal."

"Yeah," Morgan said.

"A good plan, Morgan," Jake said, "but just how do we get them split up, if what you say happens."

"It'll happen, you can count on it and getting them split up is going to be your job, Jake." Jake frowned and looked at the others. They too were puzzled. "Take four men." Morgan thought. "Sharpshooters, take four sharpshooters. Make sure you've got plenty of ammunition for them. Take four wagons and load as much dynamite as you can. I want you to ride like hell for the Cargo Muchacho." He smiled. "You're going on a treasure hunt."

Throughout the night and in the hour before sunup, the quietest one of the group had been Estralita Peralta. Now, she came forward. She moved to the table and placed on it the pistol she owned and the parchment map and plat map of the town. She turned to Tammy Winfrey. "Do you have your pistol here?" Tammy frowned, looked at her brother and then nodded. "Get it, please." Tammy complied.

"Lita," Morgan said, "we're losing time."

"Why not make Jake's treasure hunt the real thing?"

"What? What the hell are you talking about? We don't have the time to look for the fourth pistol grip right now."

"We don't have to look for it, Morgan," she said, "I know where it is, exactly."

The others moved closer and Morgan moved to the desk. He gave Estralita a studied look and glanced down at the map. "Okay, explain."

"The letters, the M and the C. They had us all going. It was so simple. M and C could be nothing else but Marin and Carbona but we were wrong. Simple it is but so simple, we tried to make it difficult." She pointed to the city may. "There, that spot." She looked up. "What stands there?" Everyone thought but it was Felisa Marin who answered.

"It is the church, Our Lady of the Mountain."

"And in front of the church," she asked. Felisa thought, looked down and then said, "My God! It's the statue!"

Morgan thought. "Mary and the baby Jesus?"

"Madonna and child," Lita said, "M and C."

# 15

The fourth pistol grip reposed in the hollowed base of the Madonna and Child statue. Together, the four grips revealed a surprise of their own. Peralta had indeed sent the groups of boys out to bury the gold in small amounts and at all four points of the compass but he did not leave it so.

Peralta reclaimed eighty percent of the gold later, leaving only smidgens of it at the original four sites. The major portion was buried in the narrow confines of a canyon called El Cavidad, the cave or hole. It's location was well known to the longtime residents of the area and to the many Peralta treasure seekers over the years. It was considered inaccessible. It was not. A single trail led to its depths and finally to the Peralta treasure.

Even as the little band in Holtville stemmed their urge to celebrate prematurely and, instead, prepared Jake for his trip and themselves for the possible fight ahead, Morgan's prediction was coming to fruition.

It was, amazingly enough, Don Miguel Carbona who first displayed the white flag. It was little wonder Marin took so long to honor it. Carbona had been winning and Marin had been considering a withdrawal until he could reorganize.

"*Señor* Marin." Joaquin Marin got to his feet and gave Don Miguel Carbona the onceover. Finally, he extended an arm and gestured for Carbona to sit down. "We must stop our fighting. We face a mutual enemy in the *Yanqui* Morgan. It is he upon whom we should vent our wrath."

"You propose peace between us now, Don Miguel, so that we might defeat Morgan. But what of tomorrow?"

"Tomorrow we will share the spoils of victory. The Peralta treasure can be ours." Don Miguel swung his arm in a wide arc and said, "This valley and all that lives within it can be ours. Is there not enough for two?"

"There never has been before, why now?"

Carbona smiled. "Perhaps, *señor*, you and I do not share the same beliefs but hear me out and then decide. Each and every man who has sought the Peralta treasure for himself alone, has found instead, the Peralta curse. I, Don

Miguel Carbona, would rather rule half a land with half a treasure than be sole owner of a curse."

"I do not believe in curses, Carbona."

"Very well then, do you believe in Morgan?"

At Don Miguel's base camp, Judge Arlo Lunsford eyed the big white stallion just outside Carbona's field tent. Carbona had honored tradition by riding a wagon to meet Joaquin Marin.

Most of Carbona's men were on the line, at the ready against the advent of their leader's failure. Lunsford knew if he was to live, he would have to escape now. Carbona had left him in custody of Juan, the lecherous little man who had terrorized Lunsford's wife.

Juan stood just outside the tent. Lunsford knew he could not manhandle the Mexican and the judge had no weapon. Suddenly, Judge Lunsford saw the blue smoke of a cigar. He got to his feet and moved to the tent's opening. Juan turned quickly, frowning.

"I'm afraid I came off without my own cigars," he said. The judge didn't smoke. He was holding a twenty dollar gold piece between his thumb and forefinger. "May I buy one of yours?"

Juan smiled. It was a grimy toothed, drooling smile. "I have no *pesos, señor*. I would have to keep all of that."

"Of course," Lunsford said. Juan reached for a cigar and held it out. The judge took it, stretched out his hand which held the coin and then dropped it. "Sorry," he said. He looked

down and at once dropped to his knees. There
was sand and rocks and brush in abundance and
the coin had disappeared. By the time Lunsford
got to his knees, he'd already spotted it but he
put one hand over it and looked up.

Juan dropped to his own knees and Judge
Lunsford eyed the huge Bowie knife in a sheath
on Juan's right hip. They were facing each other
only a foot apart. Juan dug around in the sand.

"Be careful," Lunsford said, "you may
cover it up and we'll never find it." As he spoke,
he moved his hand slightly and tossed the coin
just to Juan's left and behind him. A moment
later, the judge said, "There, there it is." Juan
looked up and saw the judge pointing. Juan
turned to his left. The sun sparkled off the gold
coin's surface. Juan grinned, turned still more
and started to crawl toward it.

Arlo Lunsford thought the hardest thing he
had ever done in his life was to shoot a man.
When he shot Luis Carbona, he fought off his
nausea and he did not think he could ever kill
again. Now, all he could see in his mind's eye and
hear in his memory was Juan pawing Mrs.
Lunsford and her screams.

The judge reached out, grabbed the handle
of the knife and pulled, hard. Juan came up to his
knees and whirled around to face the judge. At
that moment, eye to eye, Arlo Lunsford brought
the big Bowie down from above his head in a
long sweep. Its point struck flesh just to the left
of Juan's breast bone and buried itself almost to
the hilt. Juan grunted, grabbed at the wound,

coughed a bloody cough and fell face down, dead.

Don Miguel Carbona returned to his own camp. He had made his point and, in his own mind, won the day. Joaquin Marin ordered his lieutenants to ready themselves for the attack on Holtville. Carbona would do the same. Now, once more, the gods awoke and resumed the games they play on mortal men.

Both Carbona and Marin had sent out patrols that morning to reconnoiter Holtville. Carbona's men left first and returned first, arriving almost as he returned to his camp. Juan's dead body and the Mexican's missing stallion were his first discoveries. The judge had tricked him. At first, his anger was almost out of hand but Lunsford's trick had backfired. Carbona and Marin were no longer enemies.

"The town," Carbona said, "what of the town?"

"Defended by perhaps thirty or forty men but we must attack before help comes back."

Carbona was puzzled at his man's report and statement. Help?

"What help? From who? From where?"

The man shrugged and said, "I do not know, Don Miguel, but four wagons and five men go east, there," he pointed, "toward the Cargo Muchacho. The wagons, they are almost empty. A few boxes, probably ammunition. I think they go to get more men." Don Miguel knew otherwise. Gold, not men, moved those wagons.

Carbona wasted no time. He ordered his men to ride north again but this time to watch for Marin's patrol. When they were found, Carbona told them, they were to be killed! Carbona himself rode back to Marin's camp.

"*Señor* Marin, I return with mixed news." Marin had already broken down his field tent and was about to begin his northward march.

"What news, *senor* Carbona?"

"Your own patrol was killed. A band from the town ambushed them. I ordered my men to ride to the north of the town. They have reported that the north is weakly defended. I will need two hours to position my men. I suggest you attack the south side in ninety minutes. That will draw their fire and their attention and I will sweep down upon them from behind."

"I wish to confirm what you tell me for myself!"

Carbona smiled. "Of course, *señor* Marin. If you do not find it as I have described, cancel your attack. I will hold until I hear gunfire. I have no reason to lie to you."

Marin's suspicion of Don Miguel Carbona was deeply rooted and not easily dispelled but he nodded and said, "If I find my patrol and see for myself the town's defenses, I will attack as you have suggested." Carbona smiled, waved and rode off.

Carbona issued orders to all but five of his best lieutenants. The main body of his force did, in fact, ride west and north, getting into position for the attack about which he had told Marin. Carbona himself had far different plans. His five most trusted men and ten of his best troops, led by Carbona himself, rode south and east, toward the Cargo Muchacho!

After a thirty minute march, Joaquin Marin found the truth of Carbona's last visit to him. Marin's men were lying slaughtered along the road. He doubled the men's pace and figured he would be in attack position right on schedule.

Arlo Lunsford was welcomed back with no small amount of attention. Joined, finally, by his wife, the judge reported what he had done and its result.

"I'm afraid," he concluded, "that it didn't work as I had hoped."

"The hell it didn't, Judge," Morgan said. "The only chance we ever had was cutting down some of the odds. Your plan did that for us. Now, we'll have to capitalize on it."

"I just wish," Lunsford said, "that I knew what Marin and Carbona agreed upon."

"We can't know everything," Morgan said.

Morgan, Tad Winfrey and Cy Black split up and went off to alert the men to the expected onslaught. Morgan, after a visit to the sharp shooters on the court house roof, rounded up the big Chinese, Cho Ping. He, Morgan and three other men, manhandled the Gatling gun into a new position to cover the southwest. Morgan anticipated a two pronged attack, one from the southeast and one from the southwest. He didn't believe either force marshalled against the town would take the time to move north. He underestimated Carbona's former cavalry troops.

Once Morgan was satisfied that everything that could be done was done, he returned to the saloon. He found a tearful Felisa Marin and he soon learned why from Tammy Winfrey.

"Teresa slipped away to meet her father and try to find out his plans and the agreements he made with Carbona."

"Dammit! I know she meant well, but her showing up right now could stop Marin in his tracks. If he smells a skunk we're through." Morgan poured himself a shot of whiskey and downed it. He eyed Felisa and added, "To say nothing about the danger to herself." He was thinking again of the day he'd been in bed with the two sisters and shook himself for having such thoughts at a time like this.

A few miles south, Joaquin Marin halted his troops.

"Teresa?" Joaquin Marin dismounted and ran along the road. Teresa Marin rode to meet him. She slipped from her horse into his arms and she wept. He comforted her. Slowly, she regained her composure.

"Daddy . . . I," she paused, "Felisa, she's, I . . . I killed her. She shamed us and helped the *Yanqui* dog." Teresa had always been her father's favorite and could elicit from him almost anything she wanted. Now he nodded his head in a gesture of understanding and he held her close to him.

"She is free of his spell now," he whispered "and you did what God dictated. He used your hand to strike this evil from our family."

Teresa looked up. "We must avenge her death. Morgan must die." Teresa had once loved her father very much but the death of her mother had changed him, and the fever for gold and power had made his mind sick.

"We ride now to cleanse the town of his evil and he will die and Felisa's spirit, too, will be free of him."

"They have many guns," she said, "straight ahead." Marin smiled and nodded. "Yes, my daughter, I know. Soon, we will hear them all and then Don Miguel will sweep down upon them from the north." Teresa looked up, smiled and kissed her father.

"I wish to go home now and rest. May I go home, Father?"

"Yes, of course, my daughter. I will send two men to escort you."

She shook her head. "No, please father, no. You will need all your men and I wish only to be alone." Marin hesitated but then realized there could be no harm to her behind his force. After all, Don Miguel was a long way off by now. He nodded.

Teresa rode off to the south and the troops began their northward movement again. A mile south, Teresa left the trail, wheeled her mount north and spurred it to an all out gallop. She reached a ridge a quarter of an hour later and looked down. She was fifteen or perhaps twenty minutes ahead of her father's force. It was, she knew, enough.

She made her report to Morgan and merely

smiled at his anger for the risk she had taken. It had paid off in a big way and both of them knew it. Morgan rounded up Cho Ping for the second time and with three other men, moved the Gatling gun for the last time, to the northwest quadrant.

Cy Black and Tad Winfrey both expressed concerns about the attack's coordination. Even with their knowledge and the loss of the element of surprise to the enemy, they were still faced with two fronts to cover. Morgan had already thought about it.

"We'll entice Carbona's force into attacking too soon. We're about to make a little noise of our own."

Cy grinned. "How much fireworks do you want?"

"Tell 'em to cut loose with everything they've got," Morgan said, "give me a couple of minutes worth." Cy nodded. Tad Winfrey said, "I'm going up to the roof of the courthouse and keep an eye on the results." Morgan nodded.

The barrage cut loose just eight minutes later and Tad caught Morgan on his way to the north end of town. "Thirty men I'd guess," Tad said, "headed right into the Gatling."

"Ride with me, Tad, I've got another little surprise for them. I sent a few men out last night with some dynamite." Morgan grinned. "North, a whole damned line of it about a hundred yards from the city limits."

Carbona's men rode down on the town in a

single line. They were certain that the firing they'd heard was that of Marin's attack. They were shooting as they rode in, not hitting anyone or anything and not really caring. Morgan and Tad reached the Gatling gun which was covered with a tarp and set up behind a well in the middle of the street. Morgan had put four of the best rifle shots on rooftops, two on each side of the street. A moment after Morgan and Tad arrived, the riflemen cut loose.

The dynamite went up with the inconsistency with which it was buried. Five or six sticks at a time and then one or two.

Carbona's line of men was by no means a straight line. The result was that a dozen or so of them were already inside the line of dynamite when the first of it went up. Four or five men and at least three horses died in the initial explosions. The rooftop riflemen then went to work on the harassed riders. The dozen or so who got into town, turned onto the street and Morgan yanked the tarp from the Gatling.

The deadly, rapid fire gun took a terrible toll in the opening volleys. Men on either side of the street, Morgan among them, then singled out riders with rifles. The butchery was all on one side and without Carbona's personal leadership, the attack floundered, slowed and finally halted. Seventeen men, all afoot, marched themselves into town and surrendered to five. Three or four simply fled. The balance lay dead.

South of town, Joaquin Marin cursed when he heard the first shots. He thought his point patrol had gotten careless and been spotted. As Marin pondered the possibilities, his patrol returned in force, riding in from the east!

"*Señor* Marin, Carbona has lied. We saw him and some of his men riding east. We followed them." The man pointed. "They ride to the Cargo Muchacho!"

Marin's face flushed with anger. Just then, they heard the explosions and firing off to the north. Marin was stymied.

Joanquin Marin was a meticulous man with an eye and a head for detail. As an army officer, he had been criticized only for being, perhaps, too cautious. The argument was weak since he'd never been defeated in battle. Memories flooded back to him now, however, and he came as close as he ever had to panic.

"Charge! Attack," he screamed as he drew his field saber. "Attack the town!" The line of men was not in the attack position however and the result was a lack of coordination. The men in town waited out the first scattering of Marin's force and allowed them to cross the first dynamite barrier. The second line, in nearly twice the number, was decimated by the dynamite. The first attackers reached the second line of dynamite and they too were badly bloodied.

Back in town, Lee Morgan pulled Carbona's top man into the saloon. The others were about to be stripped of their arms and ammunition when the leader spoke to Morgan.

"It is Marin" he said, "he has tricked us. We will fight for you. Put us in the line of defense and Marin will die."

"Yeah? Why don't we ask your boss about that?"

The Mexican frowned. "Don Miguel is not here. I lead. I am uh . . . the boss. Don Miguel rides to the Cargo Muchacho."

Cho Ping, almost alone, moved the Gatling gun back to the south end of town. A little at a time, Marin's men, more than eighty of them still remaining, prepared to charge and fight their way into town. More dynamite awaited them and a Gatling gun about which they knew nothing and seventeen more men than before.

No longer among the town's defenders was Lee Morgan. He had left Tad Winfrey and Cy Black in charge and he was riding hell bent for leather toward the Cargo Muchacho and the Peralta treasure. Less than two miles out of town, Morgan ran headlong into Marin's reconnaisance patrol. Five men who were charged with finding a weak spot in the town's defenses.

Morgan reined up about a hundred yards from them and assessed his situation. They were spread into a single line facing him and perhaps fifty to seventy-five feet apart. Two of them reacted quickly, drew rifles and took some shots at him. Morgan grabbed what he thought he would need, leaped from his horse and assumed a kneeling position on the sand. Shots dug up the ground around him and he watched the leader raise his arm and then bring it down in a signal to charge. Morgan shocked his attackers with back to back rifle shots which cut their numbers

from five to three. The remaining three fanned
out and dropped low to their saddles.

Morgan laid the Winchester aside. He was
more than a little familiar with the skill of well
trained Mexican cavalry. He would have to shoot
their horses to stop them. The flank riders were
to approach him simultaneously and thereby
give the center man a chance at a shot. Too, in
their scissor-like charge, the flank riders would
both be in a position to get off a shot and their
hapless victim would do well to get only one of
them.

The center man fired, Morgan raised up,
stiffened and fell. A few seconds later, the flank
riders came within a few feet of Morgan, both
sitting high in the saddle and looking down.
Morgan came up and unleashed the blacksnake
whip. The first rider took the tip of the lash
across the face and howled with pain, jerking so
violently, he lost his tenuous balance and tumbled from his horse. The second lash struck
exactly where Morgan placed it, on the second
rider's mount. The animal's flank just behind
the saddle. The flesh wasn't broken and the
animal wasn't hurt except for the shock of the
moment. It snorted, whinnied and dug both
front feet into the sand. The rider went ass over
appetite over the animal's head.

The third rider, the center man, went by the
action full speed, wheeled his horse and turned
back. Morgan whirled around, dropped the whip,
drew his Bisley and killed the man.

The Mexican with the whip-slashed face

never returned. The man who'd been dumped from his horse sustained a broken neck. Morgan recovered his gear and his horse and mounted up. Behind him, he could hear occasional explosions, the steady rhythm of the Gatling gun and a din of rifle and pistol fire. He knew the town's men were heavily outnumbered and he began to wonder if even their preparations, the turn of events and Marin's disorganization would be enough of an edge.

At the same time, he looked off toward the purple-gray ridge that was the Cargo Muchacho range and thought of Jake Ledbetter and four men who would sure as hell not be expecting fifteen Mexicans to ride down on them. "Hold the town," he said, aloud, "hold the damn town." Morgan knew he would make little difference back in Holtville. He could make all the difference to Jake. He wheeled his horse and spurred her to a hard run.

# 16

It was nearing dusk by the time Morgan arrived at the spot he recognized from the map formed by the four pistol grips. It led onto the single, narrow, rocky trail which wound its way downward into El Cavidad. During the last quarter hour of his ride, he'd had to cut his speed and he'd heard plenty of gunfire. In the rocks and gorges, determining the origin of the shots was impossible and by the time he arrived at the final trail, the gunfire had stopped.

A horse whinnied. Morgan whirled around.

"*Buenos noches,* Mr. Morgan."

"Shit!" He was looking at Joaquin Marin. Two men flanked Marin and both held guns on Morgan. "Okay Marin, you won yourself a town," Morgan gestured behind him with his thumb, "but I'm guessing you lost a treasure."

Marin smiled. "You are a formidable foe, Mr. Morgan, yes indeed, most formidable. No, I did not win a town. Many of my men were cut to pieces by your lines of dynamite and your Gatling gun but the *Federales Americanos* were the biggest surprise."

Morgan thought, 'What the hell is he talking about?'

"You look puzzled. Is it possible that you didn't know they were coming?"

"Okay, Marin, you've got me. What *Federales Americanos?*" Marin smiled. "The courts have ruled the Spanish land deeds are all legal. Those who hold them own both the land and that which is found upon or under it. Until the courts so ruled, the *Federales* could not act."

Morgan needed no pictures drawn for him as to the ramifications of that ruling. It meant Tad and Tammy's land, including the very spot where they now stood, and all the land owned and shared by Lita Peralta was theirs, free and clear.

"The troops were legally sanctioned by your American government and the state of California. Those of my men and those of Don Miguel who remain alive will be tried and perhaps hanged." He smiled. "The troops were led by your famous American Marshal, Wyatt Earp."

"Well I'll be damned. I'll be goddamed!"

"Unfortunately, Morgan, none of it benefits you. Perhaps I will lose also but behind you, down in El Cavidad, Don Miguel digs up the Peralta treasure. I will die before I let him get it and I cannot allow you to live either." Morgan eyed the two men with the drop on him. He knew what his chances were and he made his decision. He could take out Joaquin Marin before he died. He knew he was fast enough to do that.

"Father." Behind and to Morgan's right, hiding in the shadows was Teresa Marin. How she came to be there, for how long and why, Morgan didn't know. Neither did her father.

"Teresa? What . . ." Joaquin Marin looked at his daughter, then at Lee Morgan, thought back to their earlier meeting and suddenly everything came together. It was too late.

Teresa brought both arms up in front of her, cocked the pistol, steadied it and pulled the trigger. The two men flanking Marin were awestruck with the idea of a daughter gunning down her own father. Marin died instantly with a bullet through his brain. The two men's momentary distraction and Morgan's lightning speed signed their death warrants.

Teresa, it developed, had seen her father a second time that day and pleaded with him to give up the fight, save the town and go home. He promised that he would do so but she followed him. The trail ended here at the entrance to El Cavidad and a golden treasure which was forever stained with the blood of the Marin family.

"You stay here," Morgan cautioned her, "but if I'm not back by daylight, you ride back to Holtville. No questions, no last minute changes." Teresa nodded but Morgan wasn't even sure she'd heard him. After all, she had actually done what he could not bring himself to do once. She had killed her father.

The sun had to climb fairly high to bring daylight to El Cavidad. Morgan spent the night on a ledge, some fifty feet from the bottom of the gorge. When he finally woke up he got to his feet and looked into the hole below him.

"Goddam," he said, "goddam, what a sight! What a hulluva sight." Indeed it was a sight. What Morgan saw was five wagons loaded with bright, shiny metal. Gold and more gold! Hundreds of pounds of it, he reckoned. The Peralta treasure. Morgan let his eyes scan the canyon floor. He saw the body of a man, then another, then another. "Dammit!" Jake Ledbetter was sitting up, his back to a rocky wall. Next to him was a pile of gold trinkets and his Winchester and two wooden crates. Even at the distance, Morgan could see the blood on his face and where it had trickled down his nose from the hole in his forehead.

"*Buenos dias,* Morgan." Out of a small opening, not far from Jake's body, emerged Don Miguel Carbona followed by several men. "Before you act hastily and foolishly, look across the canyon." Morgan did. Opposite him, perhaps twenty-five feet below, was another ledge. It was wider than the one he was on and longer. Lined up on it were no less than ten men. All of them had rifles and they were all pointed at Lee Morgan. "You are a dead man, no *señorita* to save you now."

Morgan considered the small opening just behind him where he'd spent the night. He eyed the riflemen again. Hell, he thought, if one of them didn't get me directly, the ricochets would cut me to pieces.

"I didn't want you to be hasty, *Señor,*" Carbona shouted, "because then you would die before I could show you just how rich you've made me." Carbona gestured toward the wagons with a sweep of his hand, "These carry only the small items, the baubles and trinkets of a lost race." He motioned to one of his men and several of them re-entered the cave. In a few minutes, they began coming out, carrying stack after stack of pure gold bricks. "You see, *señor*, you see how wealthy you have made Don Miguel Carbona."

Morgan watched as the Mexican bandit disappeared again into the cave. When he reappeared he was holding up a bottle of tequila. "Come, come down and let me toast you with a final drink." Carbona waved the bottle. "Or do you wish me to signal your death now?"

Morgan's eyes were roaming the length and breadth of the narrow canyon. His eyes returned once more to the body of his friend, Jake Ledbetter. Then, they moved slightly and he said beneath his breath, "Thanks, Jake." He waved to Carbona and shouted, "I'll drink with you, Don Miguel."

Morgan heard the levers of ten rifles lock into place. If he made any move which displeased Don Miguel, he'd be cut down at once. On the other hand, if he made no move at all, he was most definitely dead. He got up from his squatting position and eyed the little hole again. "If this don't fuckin' work, Morgan," he said aloud, "you're going to hate yourself in the morning."

Morgan waved to Carbona and then to the men across the canyon. He looked down again at Jake Ledbetter and the two wooden crates next to his body. Dynamite! Morgan had to be faster and more accurate than in any gunfight. He drew, dropped, fired twice and rolled into the hole. He released his pistol and covered his head.

Don Miguel Carbona saw Morgan's moves and he even had time to follow Morgan's line of sight just before the gunman drew and fired.

*"Madre de Dios,"* were the last words ever uttered by Don Miguel Carbona. The explosions were ear shattering, first one case and then the second. Morgan could see very little opposite him except the rock wall falling away as though it was being pushed by some giant hand. The rock ledge supporting the gunmen went first but the noise of Morgan's shots and the explosions themselves drowned out the screams of buried men.

Morgan could only pray that there was no dynamite on his side of the canyon. Even then, the close quarters and unstable condition of the ancient rock walls didn't give him much room for error. He could only count on the explosions ripping away the base of the far side of the canyon. Indeed, that is what occurred but when Morgan finally got to his feet and the choking dust had settled, there was no more El Cavidad.

"Sonuvabitch!"

Between the fund raising dance held by the good people of Holtville, a Federal and a State bounty and a token gesture from Wyatt Earp, Lee Morgan earned himself a fee of $759.82. He grinned to himself, there had been a few fringe benefits.

He said his goodbyes to the Winfreys and to

Felisa Marin. Wyatt hung around Holtville long enough for them to tie on one good drunk, or Morgan anyway. Wyatt didn't drink. Part of his great fortune went at the poker tables. He stayed around Holtville for another two weeks and then he spent another two hundred of his money, on supplies.

On a sunny morning nearly two months after the affair had come to an end, Morgan was packing the last of his possibiles. A knock came at his door. He walked over, pulled it open and found himself staring into the face of Estralita Peralta.

"Well I'll be damned." He stepped back. She smiled and entered his room. "I never figured to see you again." She turned to face him.

"Why, because of the treasure?"

"Seems to me that would be reason enough."

"You did the only thing you could do. I left Holtville the very night Marshal Earp arrived. I went to Sacramento and filed my claims and those of the Winfreys. We have land and I want you to have some of it."

Morgan shook his head. "I've been paid."

"I heard what you were paid."

"Gold I'll take, land, no thanks. I've had my fill of land."

"What are your plans, Morgan?"

Morgan ran his tongue into his cheek and glanced at the floor. He looked up again and grinned, rather sheepishly. "I've got a friend back in Missouri who's a mining engineer. I kinda thought I might go spend the winter with him and then ride back out this way along around next spring."

"And do what," Lita asked, smiling, "some treasure hunting?"

"Mebbe."

"Well I had another reason for stopping to see you too. Are you in a hurry?"

"Well, some. Why?"

"I just wanted to show you how grateful I was for your help." Morgan walked over and closed the door.

"My engineering friend doesn't know I'm coming. I can be a day or two late." Lita smiled. Two days turned into five. Morgan didn't know anyone could be that damned grateful.

On the fifteenth day of January, Morgan came down for breakfast at the home of his friend, Daniel Jennings, in St. Louis. Dan said nothing but handed Morgan that day's copy of the *St. Louis Globe-Democrat*. He jabbed a finger at an item near the bottom of page one. Morgan read the headline and sub-headlines. They were all he needed to read.

> "Earthquake Rumbles Across Southern California Desert. No Loss of Life Reported and Only Minor Property Damage. Major Alterations Occur to Cargo Muchacho Mountain Range.

Morgan tossed the paper aside, looked up at Dan Jennings and said, "Sonuvabitch!"